UNHOLY INTENT

UNHOLY UNION DUET BOOK 2

NATASHA KNIGHT

Copyright © 2020 by Natasha Knight

All rights reserved.

No part of this book may be reproduced in any form or by any electronic or mechanical means, including information storage and retrieval systems, without written permission from the author, except for the use of brief quotations in a book review.

1
CRISTINA

"*Welcome home, Brother.*"

I look up at Damian. Beautiful Damian.

He shifts his gaze to mine.

"Didn't I tell you to leave the locked doors alone?" he asks me, but his voice is strange. Echoing in this dusty, forgotten place.

The music starts again. That eerie sound of piano keys played slowly, so fitting to this place, this room, this house.

My head is spinning.

The other man, Damian's *brother*, says something. His voice is similar to Damian's but off. Like his face. Wrong.

Damian tucks hair behind my ear.

I push his hand away, push his arms away. I turn

slowly. They're both watching me now, waiting to see what I'll do.

And the tune keeps playing, the chords slow. Sad.

I need to look at him.

Can they hear my heartbeat? Blood beats like a drum against my ears.

Run.

Run.

But I can't run. I meet a monster at every turn. One standing behind me. The other holding me.

He warned me about the monsters. How many more hide in this house?

"Cristina," Damian says.

I keep turning, my body still pressed to Damian's.

I've taken shelter in my enemy's arms.

He's in my periphery now. The monster. The brother. Tall, like Damian. I see the coat. It's wet. He was the man walking back toward the house. It wasn't Damian at all. What is out there that they go to see in the dead of night?

Dark hair.

Identical twins.

It's easy to tell them apart now though.

My eyes finally find the monster's eyes. My breath catches in my throat.

I remember when I was little, and I stared at Damian's damaged hand. But this? This is worse.

Much worse.

His face...I see Damian in it. In half of it. The damage on the other half, no, not quite half. It's from the corner of his eye back into his hairline, one ear gone. It's like Damian's hand, his arm.

Melted skin.

"Not as pretty as my brother, am I?" he asks too casually, tone mocking like Damian's can sometimes be.

I move to break free, to run, but Damian captures my arms. He holds me still, making me face his brother.

I want to close my eyes, to turn my face away, but I can't do either because I can't stop looking.

And as if to accommodate me, Damian's brother shifts his position, giving me the full effect of the damage.

"Let me go." It's a whispered plea because I can't make my voice work. I'm sure Damian doesn't hear me. I think my lips are moving, but even I don't hear more than my wavering breath.

Damian says something, but his words have to battle the blood thudding against my ears to be heard.

The brother grins. His gaze slides over me. The look in his eyes when he returns them to mine has me pressing my back into Damian.

He walks toward us.

A sound comes from inside my throat, a garbled choke on a scream.

It's not his face that has me terrified, though. It's the look in his eyes.

Damian won't back away and his brother just keeps coming closer. My hands grab onto Damian's. I'm pulling and scratching as his brother comes so near that I can smell the forest and the rain on him. Feel the chill coming off of him.

"Pretty," he says, raising a hand but thinking better of touching me when I cry out. "I can't help how I look, you know," he says. "Ask my brother. The fault lies with him, after all."

Damian's fault?

He does touch me then. He takes my hand, the one with the ring on it, and my legs tremble.

Damian holds me up, steadies me.

His brother drops my arm like he's tossing something away. His expression darkens chilling me through. I want out of here. I need to get away from him. I'm sure if it weren't for Damian, I'd be on the ground now. A whimpering, pathetic heap at their feet.

"Are you taking good care of her for me, Brother?" he asks.

His fingers are on my face then. Cold fingers. Cold breath. Cold heart.

And this time, when my knees give out and the music fades away I don't fight it. I give myself over to it, feel myself slip away, my vision going black.

2

DAMIAN

Cristina lies limp in my arms, head back, lips slightly parted and eyes closed as I carry her back to her room to lay her on her bed.

Once there, she opens her eyes with a start, bolting upright, almost smashing her head into mine. She claws at my arms.

"Easy," I tell her.

Seeing my brother without a warning will give anyone a shock. Hell, even with warning, it'll scare the fuck out of most.

She makes a sound, pushes against me.

I collect her wrists in my hands and hold onto her. "I said easy."

She looks around her room. Is she reassured by its familiarity? Because after a moment, she does relax a little.

I look down at her. Black smears her face and rings her eyes. She's still wearing the dress from earlier, but it's wrinkled, the hem dirty. A mess. She's barefoot and shivering all over.

I take the blanket and tuck it around her. I swear I can hear the music again. That fucking Victrola Lucas had custom-made more than ten years ago. Can't he fucking stream music like the rest of the world? He always did have a flair for the dramatic. I should have smashed the damned thing with a hammer the day he left.

"Didn't I tell you to leave the locked doors alone?"

"It wasn't locked. I saw you..." She shakes her head. "I thought..." Her forehead creases as she trails off. "But it wasn't you."

I haven't seen my brother in too many years. Identical twins, almost. His eyes are a shade darker. Like his soul. Although if you asked him, I'm sure he'd call my soul black.

"Are you all right?" I ask Cristina when her wet eyes focus back on mine.

"Where is he?"

"Don't worry about Lucas. He won't hurt you."

"He said...he asked if you'd been taking care of me for him." Her face contorts.

Something twists inside my gut at my own memory of his words. Motherfucker. "Do you want something to help you sleep?"

"What did he mean, Damian?"

"Nothing. He won't touch you."

"Touch me?" She scrubs her face with her hands.

I pull them away. "He won't hurt you. No one will." I put my thumb to her ring. "This will keep you safe from them."

"What do you mean?"

"Tomorrow, you and I will be married."

"Tomorrow?"

"No one can touch you once that happens. Not the men at that party. Not those in my family."

"But *you* will touch me." She pulls her hands from mine.

Her comment catches me off guard.

"Did…his face…did that happen in the accident?"

I nod.

"He said it was your fault. Why?"

I lock my features. "Because I was driving."

She looks confused.

"I was driving the car your father rammed into, sending us onto the path of that damned train." The train only clipped the car, but at the speed it was traveling, it was enough. I wonder if it had hit us head-on if we wouldn't have all been better off. The Di Santo family wiped from the face of the earth in one fell swoop.

She studies me for a long time.

I keep my features schooled. "I need to go. Do you need something to help you sleep?"

"One of your needles? No, thank you. Why is he here?"

"To take what's mine." I stand. "But don't worry, I have no intention of giving it to him. Of giving *you* to him." I walk to the door. "Get some sleep, Cristina."

"I don't want to marry you, Damian."

"You want to remain fair game?"

"I want to go home."

"I *am* your home. Haven't you figured that out yet?"

"I won't do it. I won't marry you."

"What are your options?"

"Just let me go."

"You're naïve, Cristina. Be grateful I've taken you under my protection."

"Grateful?"

"Yes, grateful." I walk back to her. "Look around you. You're in my house. And in this house, you have one ally and many enemies. Those men at the party? I told you what they'd do to you if they could. Who's left? Your uncle? You think he'll save you? Remember that he sat at that table too. Or maybe your young cousin. He may be good at digging up information but I'm pretty sure even you don't want him involved with men like us."

She pushes a hand into her hair, then looks down as her forehead creases.

I take her chin and tilt her face up toward mine. "Your life before me is over. There is no going back. Understand that."

"I already know that." She tugs free.

"Good."

She's quiet for a long minute. "What happens after the year?"

I study her.

"Am I going to die because your sister died?"

I step away. I need a drink.

"Is that the plan?" she pushes.

"That's not my plan."

She rubs her face, wraps her hands around the back of her neck, then weaves her fingers together tightly in her lap.

"What do you mean? Please just explain everything to me. Just tell me. I can't handle the games you're playing, Damian. I'm not in your league. I'm... God, how many days has it been? I'm already falling apart. I want to talk to Liam. I want...I want this to go away. I want *you* to go away."

"It's not going away. *I'm* not going away. You will marry me because you need me to survive this."

"Survive it how? How do I come out on the other side of this?"

I consider her and draw a tight breath in. My exhale is a sigh. "You give me what I want, and when it's time, I will let you go."

She opens her mouth, closes it again, and studies me, eyebrows furrowing. "What?"

"You heard me."

"You'll let me go?"

I nod.

"Why? Why would you do that?"

"What's the point of keeping you when I'm through?"

She winces as if I've slapped her. I hear my words. Her expression darkens, a deep distrust settling in her eyes.

"I give you my word, Cristina."

"What good is your word?"

"It's all you've got."

"And why do you need me? Let's both be clear here. You're not helping me. What is it you want from me exactly?"

"For starters, I want tomorrow. I could threaten you. I could hurt you. Hurt someone you love. I'll get what I want either way."

"Then why are you even asking?"

"Because you're right. You are completely out of your league. You have no idea who or what you're dealing with. And maybe I remember that barefoot little girl, and when I see you like this, a barefoot woman lost in this damned place, this house of monsters, maybe I don't like it. Maybe there's something human left in me after all."

Something in her eyes softens, and I see her

innocence. I see a need to believe. To trust. Doesn't she know what that does to me?

She looks away, then back to me. "Only on paper. The marriage will only be on paper."

"The marriage will be consummated."

She licks her lips and shakes her head.

I lean toward her. "Do you want me to remind you how wet you were the other night?"

"Why would you want me when I don't want you?"

I straighten, snort. "You can deny it all you want if it makes you feel better about yourself. Deep down, you know the truth and so do I. Give me what I want and when the time is right, I'll let you go. Don't, and I'll take it anyway. But you'll be mine forever. And your forever may not be that long."

Her face pales. I could have left that last part out.

I walk to the door, open it, and step out.

"Damian," she calls out.

I stop. Turn.

"Even if I agree, if I give you what you want, know that it's not a choice I'd make if I had any real options. Know that you're still forcing me. And you can deny that all you want, but deep down, you and I will both know the truth."

I grin.

Clever girl.

Maybe she isn't so far out of her league after all.

I close the door and lock it behind me.

3

DAMIAN

"Didn't realize you were back," I say, walking into the dining room where my brother turns to meet my gaze. "You should have sent a message." I take the bottle of whiskey from Lucas, grab a glass, and pour myself one.

He goes to the window and lifts the curtain to look outside. "Would you have had my room cleaned? Had a welcome party waiting with a feast ready to celebrate the return of the prodigal son?"

"No, probably not." I take a big sip keeping my eyes on my brother's back. He's so fucking dramatic.

"Didn't think so." He drops the curtain and turns to me. "Wanted to surprise you anyway."

"Timing's suspicious."

"Michela likes to keep me informed."

"I figured that much. And Dad? He keeping you informed too?"

He studies me, eyes narrowing as he takes a sip of his drink and grins. "All you have are enemies. How does that feel, Brother?"

"That's certainly not the case now that you're back, I'm sure."

We both drink, neither of us taking our eyes off the other.

He's put the weight he'd lost after the accident back on. Six feet four and built as powerfully as me. If it weren't for the scars, I'm pretty sure you couldn't tell us apart. But where my arm and torso burned, Lucas took the brunt of it to his face. He almost didn't look human for a time.

"Patching you up piece by piece, are they?" It's an asshole thing to ask, but my brother is an asshole.

He's found good doctors, I have to admit. He always was a vain motherfucker. But the damage is still there, and it must have scared Cristina half to death.

"The girl," he says, instead of answering me.

"Is mine."

"Was that the blood diamond on her finger?"

"You have a keen eye."

"One has to with you for a brother. That diamond belongs to the head of the family."

"Correct."

He finishes his drink, but I don't miss how his jaw tightens. "When's the big day?"

"Tomorrow. I'm glad you'll be here to bear

witness. I'd ask you to stand as my best man, but well, you're no one's best man, are you?"

"Fuck you, Brother."

My smile almost reaches my eyes. I turn to grab the bottle and bring it back to refill his glass and mine. "What do you want, Lucas? Why are you back?"

"What do you mean? This is my home as much as yours."

"This place isn't a home for either of us."

"If that's the case, then why did you stay? You could have walked away."

"You know that was never an option after you left. Now, what do you want?"

Moving to sit on the sofa, he's thoughtful for a long minute. Doesn't have that smug asshole expression on his face for a sliver of time.

"Do you have any idea how it feels to have someone look at you and have the reaction she had?"

I hear resentment in his words, but there's more. There's sadness. A sort of resignation.

"No, I guess you wouldn't," he says when I don't reply.

"She was unprepared."

"You think it goes better when they're prepared?"

I've thought about this. Thought about it a lot. "No, I don't."

"Well, you're right. But do you know how it

fucking *feels*?" He gestures with a nod to my hand. "You deal with that, but you can wear a glove. I don't have that luxury."

"Your doctors are good," I say. I mean it. Last time I saw him, it was a lot worse.

"Like you said, they're putting me back together piece by piece. A sort of Frankenstein." He shakes his head, mouth in a sneer. "But answer my question, Brother. Do you know what it feels like to have a woman scream when she sees your face?"

"Why don't you tell me. You clearly want to." Resentment marks my words too. That and guilt.

I should hear it, shouldn't I? I owe him that much. Because he was right in a way. It was my fault. I was driving.

And maybe subconsciously I saw my opportunity to hurt him and took it. I mean, I'd been taking the fucking hurt for as long as I could fucking remember. Would anyone even blame me?

I drink my whiskey.

No.

That's not how it happened.

And what followed the accident, I certainly never intended that.

"The Gates of Hell." He gestures toward the entrance, changing the subject. "Fitting for this hell. You've gotten better."

I nod my acknowledgment of the compliment.

I'm still waiting for him to continue with the other topic.

He stands, walks toward me. "You got everything you wanted in the end, didn't you?"

"No one gave me a damn thing. I earned it all."

"Damian Di Santo. Head of the family. A man more feared than even our father was in his day. Business is good, I hear."

"I worked my ass off to get here after Dad dropped the ball and you disappeared."

"And now you get the pretty girl, too." He goes on as if I haven't spoken.

My jaw tightens at the mention of Cristina like it didn't at those other things.

"What's it like to have it all, Brother?" he asks.

"Tell me what it feels like to have a woman scream when she sees you, Lucas."

"You don't want to know, Damian." He puts his empty glass down. "I'm tired. It's been a long day." He walks away. "Long fucking life."

"Brother."

He stops and turns back.

"Tell me."

He studies me, eyes narrowed. Resentment. Not sadness now. "You and your fiancée have a big day tomorrow. Get some sleep. You look like shit."

"Fuck you."

"You already fucked me when you drove our car onto those fucking tracks."

I step toward him. "That's not how it happened, and you fucking know it."

"How does revenge taste? That's what it was, wasn't it? For all those years you took it while you think I stood by and let it happen? While you think I wanted it to happen."

"I didn't realize the fire damaged your brain, too. The accident was caused by Joseph Valentina. And I lost as much as you did."

"No, not quite as much," he says and stalks away.

"Lucas."

He stops and turns again.

"It was us against them once. Or don't you remember?"

He snorts, and even in the dimly lit rooms, I see his pain. "That was a long time ago, Brother. You just make sure your girl stays out of my way or she's fair game, ring or not."

4

CRISTINA

I took shelter in his arms.
After seeing his brother, I felt safe in Damian's arms.

"What's the point of keeping you when I'm through?"

I groan as I make myself remember what he said, then push the covers off and get up. Something is seriously wrong with me.

I walk into the bathroom only pausing for a moment on my reflection—I've looked better—before bending down to open the cupboard under the sink. Inside I'd hidden the knife I took from the hallway. After cleaning it, I'd stored it here, and now, given the circumstances, I'd feel better sleeping with it under my pillow.

But as I look through the cabinet, which is stocked with toiletries, I empty everything onto the floor to find it missing.

I'd hidden it inside one of the boxes of tampons.

For a moment, I doubt whether or not I'm remembering clearly. I go through the cabinet again, and then all the drawers, but I don't find it. The knife is gone.

Damian had asked me about my walk the morning after. Did he have my room searched once we'd gone to the city and confiscated the knife? Was it Elise?

"Crap."

I straighten, meeting my eyes in the reflection. I really do look like shit.

Turning on the tap, I wash my face before going back into the bedroom. I test the doors to double-check they're locked before I get into bed. I can't sleep, though. My mind is racing, and that eerie tune keeps playing in my head.

Lucas Di Santo is alive and well. Sort of.

And he scared the crap out of me.

I feel superficial in a way. He was scarred in the accident that changed all our lives. But it wasn't just the damaged skin of his face and neck that scared me. It was what I saw inside his eyes.

There's a darkness inside him.

Damian has it too, but it's different with Damian. Or am I willfully blind where Damian is concerned because I'm drawn to him? Because I want him?

God. What is wrong with me?

I think about Liam. About Damian letting me see

him and giving us time alone together. He didn't have to do that. And I think about that last night in the city. When I pushed him and when he could have done anything he wanted, taken anything he wanted.

He hadn't.

He'd walked away.

"After humiliating you, idiot," I tell myself and roll onto my side.

And besides, he's taking more tomorrow. He will force me to marry him. And he will finish what he started that night. He's not walking away this time. I have no doubt.

But that's not what has me worried.

He's right that my denying that I'm attracted to him, that I want him, is a lie. Even now, I shudder at the thought of him on top of me, the feel of him, his weight, pressing against me. The idea of him inside me makes my belly flutter. I hate myself for it, too. But it's the truth, and if I lie to myself, aren't I giving him that piece of me too? He's already taking enough.

Give me what I want and when the time is right, I'll let you go.

Do I believe him? Would he let me go?

And when will the time be right? After one year? Damian chooses his words with care. I am very aware of that.

But there's something else. Something about the

way he looked when I asked him if I was supposed to die in payment for his sister's death. His father may have decided that to be my fate, but Damian has not. Maybe, like he said, there is something human left inside him.

I need to be smarter.

Better.

More cunning.

I need to be like them. I need to learn from them, from father and son.

Sons.

And sister? Where does Michela stand in all of this?

And ultimately, why does Damian *need* me? For the foundation? It's written in the foundation's bylaws that only a blood descendent can inherit The Valentina Foundation. The foundation will dissolve, and any remaining funds donated to the various charities should the Valentina line somehow end. He can't kill me, or the foundation goes to my uncle, to Liam, or even Simona.

My father was the eldest of the brothers, so it went to our line, but if I hadn't survived the accident, it would have gone to my uncle, then Liam and his kids or even Simona if it came to that. There's no risk of it dissolving.

But he needs me to keep control of it.

I roll onto my back and stare up at the lavender canopy over my bed. A vain part of me wonders if he chose it to match my eyes. He seems infatuated by them.

I groan. I have to stop being such an idiot when it comes to Damian Di Santo. And I need to find a way out of his bed tomorrow night. Not because I don't want to be there. I do. And that's exactly the problem.

Because there's more at stake than my body.

5

DAMIAN

"What the hell is that doing here?" I ask of the gown Elise is lifting out of its garment bag. The two women who have been hired to do Cristina's hair and makeup stand by and watch while pretending to unpack their gear.

"Your father thought it would be appropriate," Elise says.

I look at it. I should turn away but can't. Instead, my gaze locks on the dark stains. On the torn, charred once-white lace.

My stomach heaves.

I meet Elise's gaze. She's watching me. I take a step toward her, towering over her. She leans away.

"Do you think it's appropriate for my bride to wear the wedding gown my sister died in?" She may not have died that night, but she may as well have.

Annabel was gone. We all knew it. Machines kept her alive after the accident.

"Your father—"

"Is senile and dying and most importantly, no longer your master. Be very careful, Elise."

"Sir, I—"

"Give me your key to Cristina's room." I hold out my hand.

She clenches her hands together, unsure what to do. Elise has run this house for as long as I can remember. Even when my mother was alive, my father relied on Elise's cruelty and always had an ally in her. She ruled over my mother, too.

"Key. Now. Before I tell you to pack up your things and get the fuck out of *my* house."

She fumbles with the key on the chain. It was a mistake to give it to her. And I'll need to have the locks changed anyway. I don't trust her not to have made a copy for my father.

Lips pressed together she hands me the key.

"You make a mockery of my sister's memory. Take that thing and go."

She hurries out, and I pocket the key, then turn to the women. "Simple. I don't want her overdone."

"Yes, sir."

I find the dress I'd chosen in its box in a corner. I pick it up, carry it to the bed, and unpack it. I feel the women's eyes on me as I arrange it on the bed, thinking how appropriate it is. I set the shoes on the floor at the foot of the bed and turn to the women, who stand ready.

"Nothing underneath."

If they find that strange, they don't comment.

Giving them a nod, I walk down the hall to Cristina's room and unlock the door.

When I enter, she's just coming out of the bathroom, steam spilling out behind her, a towel wrapped around her torso and one piled on top of her head.

She stops short when she sees me and defensively puts her hands to the knot of the towel.

I look at the tray Elise brought up earlier.

"Why didn't you eat?"

"I don't have much of an appetite."

"Wedding jitters?"

"What do you think?"

It's late afternoon, and the sun is just beginning to set. I wonder if she realizes she has one of the best views of the sunset from here.

"We won't have dinner until late."

"I'll survive."

"I don't want you passing out."

"I'm not that fragile. And if you're referring to last night, that was different."

"Suit yourself. Are you ready? The women who'll prepare you are here."

"I can *prepare* myself."

"I'm sure you can, but tonight is special. It's our wedding, after all," I deadpan.

"Speaking of, isn't it bad luck for the bride and groom to see each other before the ceremony? Although I guess why stop now? Bad is the only kind of luck I've had ever since the night you walked into my life eight years ago."

"Leave the drama to my brother. Let's go."

"Where?"

"Down the hall." I go to the door and gesture for her to follow.

She slips into the closet and emerges a moment later wearing a sweater and a pair of jeans, then walks out into the hallway.

With a hand on her lower back, I guide her to the room where the women wait. I turn her to face me before I leave.

"Do I need to post a guard?" I ask in a voice low enough that only she'll hear.

"I won't go wandering around. I learned my lesson."

"I'm glad to hear it. I'll be back to take you to the chapel."

"Chapel?" Her eyebrows arch.

"Of course. I'm Catholic."

She looks confused. "Are you serious?"

"About being Catholic?"

"No, about the chapel. I mean, if you believe in

God, which I don't think you do, I'm pretty sure he'd condemn what you have planned."

I give her arms a squeeze. "Maybe you'll get lucky and I'll be struck down by lightning."

"One can wish."

She turns away and I know the moment her eyes fall on the dress because she spins back to face me, mouth open in a surprised O.

"One more thing," I say, reaching into my pocket to take out the phone. I toss it to her, and she instinctively reaches out to catch it.

She looks down at it, then up at me.

"Never gave you an engagement present. Be good, Cristina," I say and walk out the door.

6

CRISTINA

I stand there staring at the phone in my hands, not believing it. When I touch the screen, it comes to life. There's no passcode.

There's a missed call. When I check it, Damian's name pops on the screen. I look at the contact list and his is the only number programmed. He must have called it in order to save his number in here.

"Are you ready, miss?" one of the women asks.

I look at her. "Just a minute," I say and walk toward the window, turning my back to them.

I dial Liam's number. He answers on the first ring, and I instantly feel a combination of relief and elation.

"Hello?" he says again when I don't speak right away.

"Liam. It's me. Cristina."

"Cristina?"

I smile, realizing that smile feels strange on my face. Almost like I've forgotten how to do it.

"It's so good to hear your voice."

"I don't recognize the number."

"It's a new phone. Damian just gave it to me. Well, he tossed it at me and left, so I guess it's mine."

"Where are you?"

"I'm at the house in Upstate New York."

"Dad told me what's happening. Are you okay?"

I glance at the ring on my finger. "I have to be. How about you? How are you?"

"I'm all right. Worried about you."

"I'll be fine," I say, not sure I will. "Are you still staying with your mom?"

"I go on weekends. I have to be in the city for school."

"Miss?" one of the women says.

I turn to her, and she mouths that they need to get started.

"I have to go."

"Already? Can't we talk for a minute?"

"I can't right now. But I'll call you back as soon as I can."

"Cris?"

"Yeah?"

"You're really going to do it? Marry that man?"

Backing up, I slump on the edge of the bed because the reality of this hits me like a fist to my belly. I wipe my eyes with the heels of my hands.

"Miss? We need to dry your hair."

"I don't have a choice, Liam. The alternative is worse."

"How can—"

"I have to go. I'm sorry." I disconnect the call. I need to get through this evening. This night. And if I keep talking to Liam, I'm going to break down.

I steel my spine and stand, looking back at the dress.

It's black, not white. Not that I care because this wedding is a sham, but this dress and the veil are more appropriate for a funeral than a wedding.

"Are you ready?" one of the women asks as I lift the lace veil, feeling the weight of it. I wonder if that's in my head because it's a delicate lace even as dense as the pattern is.

I turn to the woman. "Yes," I say, dropping the length of it.

7

CRISTINA

It's fully dark when Damian returns more than an hour later. One of the women is finishing packing her things while the other puts the final pin into my hair to hold the veil in place. It drags along the floor behind me, and I can't help but think it'd be pretty under different circumstances.

The dress itself is close fitting made of a soft organza silk, like the white dress he had me wear to that party that wasn't a party at all. It reaches my ankles and has long trumpet sleeves and a high neck with a section of lace that matches the veil across the bodice. A dangerously high slit runs along the front of my right thigh, and with every move, I'm very aware of how naked I am underneath. Just like the other night.

Damian's request.

No, not request. Damian's requirement.

Dick.

I drop the lace of the veil I'm holding on to and look up at him as the woman steps away. She gives him a coquettish smile that makes me want to punch her.

He's wearing black on black. Fitting.

My eye is drawn to the cuff link he adjusts, a deep red jewel to match the red diamond on my ring, and in his lapel is a single blood red rose so much like the roses he sent me must once have been. This one, though, isn't dead.

It's striking, all that black and the blood red against it.

He's striking.

But tonight, so am I. And I see the impact in his eyes as they lock on mine for a long minute before sliding over me.

The idiot woman starts to talk.

"Get out," he says, cutting her off without looking away from me.

She looks shocked but recovers quickly. They both scurry, all heels and hair and perfume disappearing out of the room.

He steps toward me.

I don't back up. I lick my lips instead as I tilt my head back to look up at him. He stands so close I feel the heat of his body. Mine thrums along with the strange vibration coming off him. Almost like our bodies have their own ritual, a sort of mating dance.

He lowers his gaze to the lace bodice. The fingertips of his right hand find my hip, grazing the curve of it up over the arc of my waist. He meets my eyes before wrapping his fingers around to my lower back, the flat of his hand spanning the width of it as he tugs me close. I can feel him, feel his erection against my belly.

And I want him.

"You start something in me," he says, grinding against me. "I'm going to start it in you."

Before I can speak, he pushes me backward, so I drop onto the bed, half lying on my elbows.

He crouches down between my legs.

I look at his dark head, unable to move away. He grips a hip with one hand while with the other, he pushes the slit of the dress over and up. All it takes is a few inches to expose me, and the sudden cold makes me gasp.

Damian drags his gaze from my pussy to my eyes, then back.

I'm laid out like a feast. A feast for him.

All I can do is watch as his hands come to either side of my pussy. A little pressure and I'm open to him. He looks at me. Just looks at me. I bite my lip, but I can't close my legs. I don't want to. Instead, I feel the heat of his gaze, feel the damp between my legs.

Without a word, he closes his mouth over my clit. His tongue is wet and soft, the sucking motion making me gasp as I drop my head back and bite my lip, drawing blood.

He licks the length of me from one hole to the other, then flicks my clit with his tongue. Just when I think I can't take another moment, when I'm on the edge of orgasm, he's up on his feet, pulling me to mine.

I stumble.

He wraps a powerful arm around my lower back, cradling me, holding me to him as he looks at me with his nearly black eyes. His lips glisten, and I smell myself on him. When he kisses me, I open to him, tasting myself, and as wrong as it is, I want more.

I want him to finish what he has started more than once.

I want to come. Want him to make me come. It's not the same when it's my fingers doing the work.

He pulls back with a grin.

I'm breathless, clinging to his shoulders to stay upright.

"I'll finish you tonight." He kisses me again, then steps backward. "After I've made you my wife."

I only remember the phone I'm somehow still holding in my hand when his hand closes over mine, and he relieves me of it.

"No," I start, almost like I'm coming out of a trance.

"You'll get it back after the ceremony. It's yours. Now let's go. The vultures hunger for their feast."

With his arm around my lower back, we walk out of the room and through the house, down the stairs to the main floor where a fire burns in every fireplace and music plays from invisible speakers. Candles are lit and a meal that should make my mouth water, makes my stomach turn instead.

We walk through the dining room where we ate a few days ago and into the large kitchen where several staff are hard at work.

Damian takes off his jacket, and before I can figure out what's going on, he drapes it over my shoulders, and we're outside.

It's a clear night, colder than I've felt in a long time. I shiver even with his jacket on my shoulders and his arm around me.

I hurry to keep up in my high heels as he leads me over a path that's only recently been cleared to a small stone building in the distance. I realize it's the chapel as we near it. I can smell incense.

God. How long as it been since I've smelled incense? I haven't been inside a church in ages. Since the funerals. After those, I'd had enough of churches to last me a lifetime.

The warm glow of lights comes through the two windows at the front and the deep red stained glass above the door. It's the crucifixion scene.

Someone begins to play the piano inside.

Damian climbs up the stairs, taking my hand to draw me along with him as my attention is absorbed by that window. When he pushes what appears to be an ancient door open, I can make out that the pianist is playing "Ave Maria."

All the faces inside turn to us. To me.

Damian slips his jacket off my shoulders and draws the lace over my head to cover my face, skewing my view. Shielding me from them. When he pushes a small bouquet into my hand, I have no choice but to accept but wince instantly and drop the flowers.

Blood red roses litter the floor at my feet, their thorns uncut. I look at him, and he just watches me. I want to ask him why he would do that. But I look down again and remember the dead roses that littered the marble floor of my uncle's house.

Blood on white marble. Blood on stone. Always blood with him.

I touch my finger to his mouth and smear the drop of blood over his lips. I don't know why I do this. Don't know what I expect.

He licks his lips, and I think he likes the taste of it. The taste of my blood.

The music changes to a bridal march. How out of place.

I turn again to face the altar where, through the pattern of the silk, I see the waiting priest in all his robes. In the front pew sits a woman and a young boy. Michela and her son, I think. Michela dressed in black with lace over a part of her face, too. She doesn't smile, but the little boy is up on his knees in the pew, arms on the back of it and smiling wide at me. He's the only normal looking one in here.

Across the aisle sits Lucas, the good side of his face to me, and I can't help but shrink away.

And at the front of the church is the old man in his chair, a heavy blanket draped over his legs. The man who was with him last time—what was his name—is standing off along the wall nearest him.

What a strange gathering we make.

I feel a little sick when the march begins anew, but when I take a step back toward the door, Damian catches my arm.

This is wrong.

This place.

These people.

This house of God?

All I feel is hostility alongside my own fear.

I make a sound, a small whimper.

Damian pulls me forward, and I don't know why I resist. I said I would do this. I made up my mind. But I don't want it. And the closer we get to that altar, all I can think is—this isn't a funeral dress at all, but one for a sacrifice.

And I'm already bleeding.

I know there's no getting away, but still, I struggle.

He must have known I would. He just keeps on walking, hand like a vise around my arm. I'll have bruises in the shape of his grip tomorrow.

Does he care? Would he?

We walk toward the two kneelers set side-by-side before the priest. Damian forces me down to my knees, then follows. I'm surprised he kneels. Maybe he does believe in God. His left hand engulfs mine, and with the right, he makes the sign of the cross.

The priest begins.

I'm shaking and I feel faint. Maybe Damian was right. I should have eaten something.

I turn to look at him. He's looking straight ahead, his beautiful face set and hard as if carved from stone.

I look beyond him to his father whose face is openly hostile. Turning to see Michela, I try to avoid looking at Lucas, whose eyes I feel burning into my back.

The priest prattles on and on. I only hear one word, obey, as my heart races until everything goes quiet. He and Damian and everyone stare at me. Waiting for me.

It's my turn to speak.

"Say I do," Damian instructs.

I look back at him through the veil. I think about my uncle and Liam and Simona and my life before. My life now.

I think of that line of demarcation I felt like a

physical thing the moment I closed the apartment door behind me on the night I tried to escape my destiny.

That's not when my life's course was determined, though. That was almost a decade earlier when I was just a little girl. When he was already a man.

The shaking grows worse.

Damian wraps a hand around the back of my neck and squeezes. He leans toward me and through the lace I feel his breath at my ear.

"Don't make me take it. Remember what I told you."

I have no doubt he will take it. I look from him to the priest, and I say the words.

"I do."

I say them, and I seal my fate. Not that it was ever up to me.

A moment later, it's Damian's turn and then come the rings. He reaches into his pocket and slides mine onto my finger. This one doesn't hurt, at least. It settles against the engagement ring, the thorns locking into the holes on the thick band, the set complete. Thorns hidden but there. Always there.

He holds his hand out to me, and in his palm, I see a black band.

My turn again.

With a trembling hand, I take the ring. I look up at him, at his wolf-eyes. He's waiting for me, but this part doesn't matter. It's already done. I said the words.

I slide the ring onto his finger, and strangely, it's like I'm sealing his fate too.

The priest pronounces us husband and wife, and Damian lifts my veil to kiss me.

I don't close my eyes and neither does he. I still taste myself on him. And then we're on our feet, Damian pulling me up by my wrist. No one is smiling or throwing rice as the pianist plays a happy tune that doesn't belong in this place or to these people or even to me. We walk out of the chapel and when Damian lifts me in his arms and carries me back to the house, I don't fight him. I don't do anything.

I'm in shock, I guess.

Trembling with cold.

This changes things.

This changes everything.

How did it get to this point? How did we?

I'm so lost in thought that I don't register the warmth of the house. I barely notice when Damian whips the covers off the bed and sits me down. I blink, looking around.

This isn't my room.

Damian pulls my veil off. It hurts because he doesn't undo the pins first but drags them off along with the veil tugging at my hair. He's not smiling anymore. Not even grinning his wicked grin.

He walks away from me to pour two glasses of whiskey. He hands me one and swallows his completely before I've even lifted the glass.

I don't like whiskey, but tonight, I'll drink it like water.

Damian does, too. And he doesn't seem any happier than me. Any more victorious. He sits on a chair across from the bed and watches me like he's done before.

"You belong to me. Even before this, you belonged to me."

I don't speak. What am I supposed to say to that?

"Come here, Cristina." He sits up, motioning for me with two fingers. He widens his stance to make space for me to stand between his knees.

I get up and go to him. To my husband.

He leans forward, takes the empty whiskey glass dangling from my hand, and sets it aside. He looks me over.

My belly quivers. I'm not sure if it's the whiskey or his eyes on me.

Everything is still for a long minute and so deadly silent. But then he takes hold of the dress at either side of the long slit. I let out a scream when he rips it up to my belly.

"Shh." He grips my hips and tugs me closer. Without another word, he finishes what he started before our strange wedding.

He drags me so close I have to bend to place my

hands on his shoulders. He clamps his mouth over my sex, hands shifting to my ass, kneading it, pulling me open as he devours me. His tongue and teeth are wet, so wet, and when I cry out as I come, I weave my hands into his hair. I'm holding him to me, hips spasming as something leaves me, something heavy and weighted melting out of me as I come on his tongue and I scream his name.

His.

I'm his.

But I already knew that.

When it's over, and I've gone limp, he slides me down over him. My knees hit the rough carpet covering cold, unforgiving stone and all I can do is stare up at him as I try to catch my breath.

He wipes the corner of his mouth with his thumb. The way he does it and the way he looks at me, it's humiliating and arousing all over again.

He takes my face into his hands and mine close over the backs of his. His lips are wet, face smeared with me. And he kisses me hard, kisses me like he owns me.

But he does. He's told me as much.

When he draws back, he looks at me again, then lifts me to my feet. Strangely, he unzips the dress rather than ripping it the rest of the way off. It pools at my feet as he picks me up, carrying me to his bed.

I'm naked when he lays me down, watching as he undresses, removing his cuff links and setting them aside. Undoing a few buttons at the top of his shirt before pulling it over his head, he never stops looking at me. Doesn't speak a word as he undoes his belt and his pants, pushing them and his briefs off. I see him for the first time, fully naked. I've felt him before, but I've never seen him.

I back up a little on the bed. I lick my lips as the muscles of his belly and thighs tense. Then he walks toward me, arms powerful when he climbs up onto the bed before grasping one of my ankles and dragging me toward him.

"Damian…"

He lays his weight on me, not all of it though, some of it on his elbows on either side of my head.

I don't know what to do with my hands, but when I feel him between my legs, I tense and try to pull away.

"Shh, relax." One hand closes over the top of my head. He leans his face down to kiss my forehead, my cheek, my mouth. He touches my scar, traces the part on my chin, my lip.

His eyes are open, watching me, and all I can do is watch him back.

His other hand snakes down my side to close over my left thigh, winding down to my calf. He draws my leg up.

"I'm not ready," I start, hands flat against his chest.

He slides the hand from my thigh to my pussy

and rubs my clit. I'm so sensitive already, and it feels so good.

"You're ready, sweetheart."

I wrap my hands over his shoulders as he slides his hand back to my leg, opening me wider. I swallow hard because I'm scared. I never thought I'd be scared.

I don't realize I'm crying until he leans down and licks that tear, then kisses my cheek.

"You're especially beautiful when you cry."

"And you like to make me cry."

"Look at me. Just look at me."

"I'm scared." As I say it, my shoulders shudder, and I feel myself curl into him.

Into him. Not shrinking away from him but curling into him.

What the fuck is wrong with me?

"It has to happen. You know that."

I shake my head, turn away.

He touches me with a gentle hand, bringing my face back toward his.

"Did you like my mouth on you?"

"I—"

"No lies. Not now. Not in bed." The way he says it, it's strange. He's not mocking or manipulating. I think. "Tell me the truth, Cristina. Did you like my mouth on you?"

I nod.

"I liked my mouth on you, too. And I want to be

inside you. I want to feel you. I want to feel you come on my cock. And I want to come inside you."

I shudder at his words, my stomach tied up in knots, in anticipation.

"I *need* to feel you, do you understand?"

I don't. I understand that he *wants*, but I don't understand that he *needs*.

"There's something about you, Cristina, and I need it."

He moves his hips, and I feel his length slide between the lips of my pussy. I gasp.

"You look at me, understand? You don't look away."

I nod, bracing myself. My hands close on his shoulders as his hand slides to my leg once more, lifting it, opening me.

I hold my breath when I feel him at my entrance, and I watch his eyes as he begins to push inside me. He's being careful. I can tell. I know if he wants to, he can tear me in two, but he's being careful.

"Fuck," he groans, dipping his head down as he pushes in a little, stopping when I tense. "You're so fucking tight."

He brings his eyes back to mine and kisses me. A deep kiss, his tongue invading my mouth like his cock is invading my sex. I close my eyes momentarily as he claims a little more of me.

When he pulls back his eyes are almost black,

and I know it's taking all he has not to thrust hard into me.

He moves slowly back and forth, stretching me, and I know when he's reached my barrier. I feel it. I tense, panicking until his hand is on my face, caressing my cheek.

"Shh. It's okay. It's for me, don't you know that yet? For me to take."

"Damian—"

"You feel so good. So fucking good."

I swallow. It's coming. I know it.

He takes my hand and puts it on his shoulder. "Look at me. Don't look away. I want to watch you."

I nod, and his next thrust sends a shiver of pain through me. I gasp. The sensation is strange, painful, then warm and wet.

I'm bleeding again.

"God…fuck." He shifts his grip to my shoulder and both hands tighten. He holds me still and begins to fuck me. He's still holding back. Or trying to at least.

"It hurts."

He dips his head and I take more of his weight. Sweat drops from his forehead onto my cheek. He looks at me again, intense and different, like he's seeing me differently too. He kisses me and I kiss him back. He tastes good. Like whiskey and sex.

His thrusts come harder, more frantic, and I swear he grows thicker inside me. Thicker and then throbbing as he stills. I can feel him. I feel him come. I feel him fill me up as he empties inside me, eyes locked on mine, my name a groan on his lips.

And when he slides his hand between us and finds my clit, I come again. I come with him inside me, with the pain cutting me, with blood warming my thighs. I come again and I cling to him.

Even as I hate myself for it, I cling to him, my enemy.

This monster who doesn't hide in the dark. The one in whose bed I'll sleep.

My monster.

8

DAMIAN

Fuck.

Her cunt cradles my cock, throbbing around it.

Sweat drips from my forehead as I raise my head to look at her. Her nails loosen on my back. I'm sure she's broken skin, but it's the least I deserve.

She's fucking beautiful when she cries. More so when she comes.

I wipe away a tear with my thumb, then kiss her cheek. Her soft mouth.

When I slide out, I can feel her tense, and I look down at the mess between us.

Blood on her belly. Blood on her thighs. On mine. On my dick.

Blood on the white sheets of my bed.

I smell it, too. Like rust. When cum slides out of her, she tries to close her legs and pull away. I grab one thigh to stop her, almost hard again at the thought of my cum inside her. Mixed with hers. Mixed with her virgin blood.

Sitting up, I push my hair back and look at her. She shivers, so I grab the blanket to pull it over her.

"Are you okay?"

She only nods once, and I wonder what she's thinking, what's going on behind those secretive violet eyes.

"It won't always hurt," I say.

"We won't be doing it again, so it doesn't matter."

I snort, get up. We will most certainly be doing it again. I walk into the bathroom, wash my dick and my hands, then wet a towel with warm water and return to her.

When she sees the towel, she shakes her head and tries to sit up, wincing when she does.

"I can do it," she says, trying to take the towel.

I push her hand away and sit beside her. "Rest for a minute."

"Damian, I can…" I push her legs apart, but she resists, trying to tug my arm away. "It's embarrassing. Please."

"You're mine. I take care of what's mine. What's embarrassing about that? And as far as not fucking you again, well, I can tell you we will be fucking again and often. Now lie back and relax."

She lies down and looks away, her cheeks pink.

Opening her legs a little wider, I clean her belly

first, then her thighs, and finally between her legs. She sucks in a breath at that and I think I should have been gentler. Gone easier. God knows I tried but only partly succeeded.

"We're expected for dinner, so we won't have time to shower."

"Dinner? With your family?"

I start to get dressed while she sits up, holding the blanket to her.

"Your family too now, sweetheart."

"I'm not...Did you see how they looked at me?"

"No one will hurt you."

"They want to kill me, Damian."

"They're going to have to learn to live with that want because I won't allow them to hurt you." I walk to the door that connects my room to hers. From her closet, I choose a dress for her to wear. When I return, she cocks her head to the side.

"Your room's next to mine? They adjoin?"

"It was convenient. Get dressed."

"I don't want to eat with your family."

"You're going to have to get it over with. You live here now."

"Please!"

Leaving my shirt half-buttoned, I go to her and tilt her chin upward. She tries to tug free, but I tighten my grip.

"Do you appreciate your new phone?"

"What are you going to do? Give me something

then threaten to take it away every time you want me to do something awful?"

"Marriage is a give and take, Cristina. I gave you a phone. Now you give me something."

"Please don't bullshit me about marriage being a give and take. All I've seen is you taking. And besides, this is a sham."

She tries to tug free again, but when I don't release her, she slaps at my arm.

I catch her wrist, pulling her to her feet, and tug her toward me.

"Did you come tonight?"

"Get off me."

"Did you come?"

"Fuck you."

"Twice. You came twice."

"Fuck off, Damian."

"Don't push me. Didn't I already tell you that?"

"Let go of me. I'm not going to your dinner, and as far as marriage being a give and take, you already took far more than you gave!"

"Be. Careful."

"What's the matter? The truth not really something you're comfortable with?"

I grit my teeth, count to ten, and release her. "Get dressed." I walk away, picking up my jacket.

"I'm not going," she says, and when I turn to her, she sprints for the still open connecting door.

I catch her before she makes it, pushing her up against the wall. I hold her there by her arms.

"Get dressed or I'll take you down naked."

"You wouldn't dare."

I raise my eyebrows. "No? Do you really want to test me?"

She watches me. She knows I mean it. "Why do you want me to do this?" she asks, frustration making her voice sound higher. "They hate me, Damian."

"And that's exactly why. You need to be strong. They can smell weakness, Cristina. They can smell fear. It's what they want, and it's coming off you like you bathed in the stuff."

Her shoulders slump as I ease my hold on her. Her eyes fill up with tears, morph into that color of sunrise when she's about to cry.

Fuck.

"I'll be there with you. I won't leave you alone with them."

"I don't have a choice, do I? Just like the wedding. Just like that." She gestures to the bed with her eyes.

"No, you don't," I say, although that last part bothers me.

"Let me go. I'll get dressed in my room."

"Fine." I let her go and pick up her dress. I hand it to her.

She disappears into her bathroom, emerging ten minutes later. She's rigid as I take her hand and lead her downstairs where everyone is gathered, drinks in hand, the music and the mood dark.

My sister is the first to stand when we enter, her martini glass half-empty. She approaches with a strange grin on her face, something about her different.

I only realize what it is when she's standing directly in front of Cristina.

Mother. Fucker.

"Welcome to the family," she says, leaning toward Cristina, who is an inch taller than her, and kissing her on the cheek.

She shifts her attention to me. "Congratulations, Brother," she says and kisses me the same way she kissed Cristina.

Judas.

Michela smirks, then makes a point of pausing as she turns before walking away.

Cristina gasps.

Because for the first time since her return to the house, penniless and desperate, Michela is wearing a backless dress.

And the silvery lines that crisscross her skin display my shame.

Fuck.

I see Cristina's shocked expression in my periphery as her eyes lock on my sister's skin.

Michela resumes her seat and takes a sip of her

martini, her smile wide. Looking like a fucking hyena.

My brother gets to his feet.

Did he know she'd do that? Did he orchestrate the spectacle?

I give him a warning glare, but he only has eyes for my wife.

My wife.

I feel Cristina tense and I know it's taking all she has to stand still.

My brother takes his time, making a point of looking her over. The expression on his face makes me fist my hands, squeezing Cristina's. If I let go of her, she'll run screaming from this house of horrors.

Lucas stands a little too close. His eyes move a little too territorially over her.

My wife.

My fucking wife.

"Welcome to the family, sweetheart," he tells her.

She leans away as he leans toward her, but instead of kissing her cheek, he kisses her mouth.

And I lose my fucking shit.

I pounce taking hold of my brother's throat. His grin eggs me on as I back him into the wall and smash his head against it.

"*My* wife, bastard. *My* fucking wife. You touch her again and I will take off the other half of your fucking face!"

He glares at me, that grin gone, only hate remaining.

"I'm willing to share," he says.

"I'm going to fucking kill you." I draw one arm back to smash my fist into his face, but someone grabs it.

"Rules, Lucas," my father's voice comes out thick from years of smoking.

It's Johnny who's got my arm. I jam my elbow into his ribs.

Just as I'm about to punch Lucas, I hear my nephew cry out.

I stop.

Fuck.

I hadn't seen him.

I turn to find Bennie hugging Michela, face buried in her skirt.

When I look back at Lucas, he smiles at me, adjusts his suit, and glances beyond me where I can see Cristina is standing, hands on the antique table behind her for support.

Elise enters the room with the sheet in her hands. I wonder if she was standing outside my door listening to me fuck my wife. She walks over to my father and I see Cristina's face morph into one of horror and humiliation. Elise holds the bloodied sheet out for him and everyone to see.

My father makes a sound. I'm not sure if he's pleased or not.

Something shifts in the room.

Lucas swallows his drink, looking from the sheet to me. "You win this round, Brother. She's yours in the eyes of God."

"Am I supposed to believe that will stop you?"

"Stop your goddamned fighting. You know the rules, both of you. Lucas, you don't touch her now."

Lucas raises his whiskey to his mouth, and as casual as he tries to appear, I see how his knuckles have gone white around the glass.

"Careful you don't smash that," I tell him, walking to the bar and pouring two whiskeys. I carry one back to Cristina.

She takes it and swallows a gulp. I didn't realize she liked the stuff, but I'll need to watch her. Pretty sure she can't hold as much liquor as she may want to drink right about now.

My father rolls himself toward Cristina.

I put a hand at her lower back to keep her from bolting.

"You didn't like my gift?" he asks her.

She looks from him to me and back. "Gift?"

"Annabel's dress. Something old and borrowed," he says.

"What?"

"Nothing," I tell her. I turn to my father. "Welcome her and move on." I hate this next part.

"Come here, girl."

Cristina looks at me with horror in her eyes.

I nod.

"I said come here," he commands. I'm surprised he still can, in his diminished state.

"Damian..." She's shaking her head.

"Just get it done," I say quietly enough only she can hear.

"What—"

I'm about to take hold of her, to push her to him, wanting this over with. But then, with a strength I don't imagine him to have, he shoots an arm out and grabs her wrist.

Cristina's whiskey glass slips to the floor and crashes against the stone as she lets out a little scream. She's trying to twist her arm free, but he tugs her toward him.

"Be still," he tells her as she struggles.

She has to put her free hand on the arm of the wheelchair so as not to fall over.

He looks her straight in the eye, their faces inches apart. "Welcome to the family, girl," he says, and kisses her cheek.

When he releases her, she stumbles backward.

I catch her arm as she wipes off her face.

My father rolls his chair out of the room. Johnny follows and they disappear around the corner.

Good, at least he won't be staying for dinner.

Cristina wipes her eyes, trying to hide her tears. I'm sure she doesn't want this bunch to see her cry.

Her chest heaves with her breaths, and I imagine her heart is racing.

"Bennie," Michela says.

Bennie turns to face Cristina and I'm not sure who's paler right now. I make Cristina turn to me, take her face into my hands, wiping smudged eyeliner off her cheek. "Get it together. You're almost done. He's a boy, younger than Simona. Then you can go upstairs."

She nods frantically, sniffling and wiping her eyes and nose. She's about to crack.

"Go on," Michela urges my nephew.

He looks up at her, then slowly makes his way to Cristina.

Bennie reaches into his pocket and pulls out a crumpled piece of paper. He's about to cry too.

Fuck.

Why the fuck did we do this in front of him?

And why did I let Lucas get to me?

"What's that, Bennie?" I ask, trying to make my voice sound light.

He stares up at Cristina who sniffles, turning her face away. She can't keep up with the tears.

"I made a drawing for her." He gestures to Cristina.

"Look at that, Cristina," I say to her. "Isn't that nice?"

She nods, crouching down to take the drawing. "You made that for me?"

He nods but looks frightened.

"Thank you," she says.

"Bennie," Michela calls out.

He turns to her, then back to Cristina. "Welcome to the family," he says and leans in to give her the tiniest peck on the cheek before running back to his mother.

When Cristina stands, I give her a nod, and without a moment's hesitation, she disappears around the corner, heels clicking as she sprints up the stairs.

9

CRISTINA

I take a chair into the bathroom and lodge it under the doorknob, hoping it will keep out anyone who might try to come in. I can't get this dress off fast enough. Can't get under the burning hot water of the shower soon enough to scrub off their hands, their kisses.

I've never felt so humiliated in my life. And I've never felt so disgusted.

I want to peel my skin off. I swear I can still smell the old man's breath on me. Death and hate. That's what he smells like.

Lucas kissing me on my mouth? I can't even begin to understand what he was thinking. Then their conversation about rules after Elise showed them the sheet?

I scrub my face, pressing the heels of my hands into my eyes.

God. She showed them the sheet.

I don't understand.

Even under the hot flow of water, I'm shaking. Freezing. I switch it off and dry myself with a towel, then put on the thick robe hanging behind the door.

I dislodge the chair, walk back into my room, and take a deep breath in, forcing it out slowly.

The phone. It was in his pocket. Did he put his jacket on before going downstairs? I can't remember.

I open the door between our rooms tentatively but find it empty. A lamp shines on the nightstand at the far end of the freshly made bed. I guess Elise did that before taking the bloody sheet downstairs.

Did he know she'd do that?

And what if I wasn't a virgin? What would have happened then?

The whole thing makes me nauseous.

I find Damian's jacket hanging off the back of a chair. Grateful for that, I hurry to it, patting the pockets until I find the one with the phone. I slip my hand inside, relieved when I lift it out and see it's mine.

Upon my return to my own room, I spot Damian's bottle of whiskey. Without hesitating, I grab it by the neck and hurry back to my room, closing the door behind me.

I don't like whiskey and have never been a big drinker, but tonight is a good time to start.

Twisting off the lid, I take a sip directly from the

almost full bottle before setting it on the floor. Sitting down beside it, my back against the bed, I hold my hands out in front of me.

They're shaking. I'm trembling.

I look at the phone, my one solace. Although it's late, I dial Liam's number.

The phone barely rings once before he picks up. I'm not surprised. He rarely sleeps.

"Cristina?"

"Hey." There's a long pause as I try not to cry. "You weren't sleeping, I guess?" I ask, feeling my voice tremble.

"Sleep is overrated. Are you okay?"

I nod, wanting to say I am, but I'm not, and I can't really speak for a long minute.

Tonight broke me a little. Not the wedding. Not even after, in Damian's bed. He was gentle. Or tried to be. As gentle as a man like him can be, I think. I do believe he was taking care with me.

But then after? What happened downstairs broke something inside me. Broke the hope inside me.

"I don't think I can do this." I drop my head into my knees.

"Cristina. Fuck. Talk to me."

"It's done."

He's quiet for a long minute. "You had no choice. You have to do whatever it takes to survive now, Cristina. Whatever it takes."

"He said he'd let me go if I give him what he wants. That's why I did it." I feel ashamed to tell him. I feel weak. I shake my head, force my tears back. "His family...they're all here, and they hate me, and..." My voice breaks into a sob.

"Listen to me, Cristina."

Unable to speak, I nod through a choked breath, but he can't see that.

"Are you listening? Are you still there?"

"I'm here."

"You can't let them get to you. You need to be strong."

"But I'm not strong, Liam."

"Tell me again what he said. Word for word." When I don't reply, he fills in for me. "He said he'd let you go?"

"Yes."

"Good. That's something. Did he hurt you? Tonight, I mean. Did he make you—"

"No." Is it a lie? He didn't make me do anything. But I feel too ashamed to tell Liam that the marriage has been consummated.

He exhales in relief. "Is he cruel to you?"

"Yes. No, not cruel, no."

"Good. The rest of them don't matter. He's the one you have to focus on. He's the one who decides."

"I'm so scared."

"He let us see each other. That's something, Cristina. He did that for you."

"No, he didn't. He wanted something from me."

"He can take anything he wants. He did it *for you*. You have to think about that. Focus on that."

"What do you mean? How?"

"I mean he's human. He has chinks in his armor, and you're going to need to use his weaknesses against him. Against them all."

I straighten, feeling a little better.

He's right that Damian did what he did for me, for some strange reason. I don't know why he doesn't just take. And I don't believe him that he feels badly about me and has since that night he intercepted me in the hallway when my father was killed.

"He hates his family too," I say. "I know it. I see it. Feel it even. And I think they hate him."

"Good. Then you'll use that against him too. You'll get close to him. Make him care about you. Make him trust you."

"He won't care about me."

"He already does."

No. That's not right. "I don't understand what he wants. Why he'd go against his family and let me go."

"He and his brother haven't been close in a long time. Since they were teens from what I'm learning. His sister, Michela, she ran away to get married and only returned to the house recently after her husband died. And only when she was destitute.

And the father, he has cancer. I'm surprised he isn't dead already, considering."

"He's a terrible man. Evil like that doesn't die."

"I do know that Damian was very close to his mother and sister, both of whom he lost in the accident."

"But wouldn't that only make him hate me more?"

"He's a man, Cristina."

"What does that mean?"

"Do I have to spell it out?" he pauses, and I can almost feel him roll his eyes. "You're a beautiful woman. I know guys. He has a soft spot for you. A weakness. You have to focus on that."

"I don't think that's right."

"Trust me. I've seen how he looks at you."

"Okay." I don't really know if I believe him but it gives me a little strength, at least.

"Did you know he was driving the night of the accident?"

"I just found out."

"I wonder if his father blames him in some way too, in addition to blaming your father."

"That would explain at least in part why they are how they are. Lucas blames Damian for sure. He made a comment about it."

"Listen, I'm going to do some more digging here. Can I call you back?"

"Yes. But don't leave a message, just in case. He

just gave me the phone and I don't know if he'll take it back."

"All right. You try to get an idea of his timeline and what he wants exactly. Because he has something specific in mind. I'd bet my life on it."

I nod just as a soft knock comes on the door.

Startled, I gasp and turn to watch the door open.

It's not Damian. He doesn't knock.

I'm surprised to see Michela peek her head in. I get to my feet, but she puts her hand up, palm toward me, when she sees I'm on the phone. Then she backs away.

"Wait!"

She does.

"I have to go, Liam."

"Are you all right?"

"Yeah. I'll be okay. I'll talk to you soon." I disconnect the call and Michela looks behind herself before slipping inside. She's holding a small box.

"What do you want?" I ask her.

She glances around the room.

"He's not here," I say.

"I wanted to make sure Elise wasn't lurking."

I fold my arms across my chest, remembering that this is the woman who lured Simona into her car. Who essentially kidnapped her.

She looks me over, eyes the bottle of whiskey on the floor but doesn't comment.

"Are you okay after that spectacle?" she asks finally.

"No, not really."

"I'm sorry you had to go through that."

"Why would you say you're sorry? You were a part of it."

"I have to do what they tell me to do."

This confuses me, but I refuse to care about this woman.

"Here," she says, holding out the box.

"What is it? A welcome to the family gift?"

She shakes her head. "Protection."

I just watch her.

"Take it."

The box is plain, but when I open it, what I find inside surprises me. It's a switchblade.

"What is this for?"

"Like I said, protection. I know what my brother's capable of."

"Which brother?"

She smirks. "As if you need to ask. I saw the bloody sheets. I'm sure he took pleasure in that."

I feel my face burn but don't reply. Something about her visit rubs me the wrong way so I don't tell her he didn't hurt me anymore than anyone else would have the first time.

It's not only that I don't trust her. I don't like this woman.

I set the box aside and take the hilt of the small

switchblade in my hand. I touch the tip.

"Careful," she says.

It's sharp. Deadly.

I look at her. "Why are you giving me this?"

She turns around, showing me her back, and I swallow. "This is how Damian welcomed me home a few years ago."

Like earlier, I gasp at the sight, and take in the slightly raised lines of skin. There must be a dozen on her back.

She turns to face me again. "They go all the way to my ankles."

My stomach turns.

"Why would he do that?"

"Because in his eyes, I betrayed the family when I ran off with the man I loved. Bennie's father. It's all about the family to him. To all of them."

"But you hate each other. Anyone can see that. You all hate each other."

"That's not true. It's Damian who sows hate. You need to be careful with him."

"I think I need to be careful with all of you."

She gestures to the knife in my hand. "I wouldn't give you that if I had any intention of hurting you, Cristina."

"You took Simona."

"Because he made me. I would never have done that to any child. I'm a mother, Cristina. And I didn't hurt that little girl."

"You scared her."

"I know." She looks down momentarily. "And I'm sorry about that."

For some reason, I believe her. Maybe because she's a mother too. Or maybe it's those lines on her back. She's not lying about those.

"Why did you come back here? To this house?"

"Bennie's father died. I had to. I had nothing and Bennie was just a baby."

Her eyes glisten and I can't help but feel for her.

"I couldn't make it on my own. We'd be on the street and I couldn't do that to my son."

"Damian hurt you like that?"

She nods.

"Your father asked if he'd welcome me like he had you."

"Like father, like son. Just be careful. You can't trust anyone in this house."

"Does that include you?"

"I'm a victim too. Just like you. Just like my mother. All women are to them. Everyone but that bitch Elise. You watch her too. Just watch your back." She walks to the door. "I need to go before he sees me. Hide it from him, or he'll punish me again, okay? Promise me."

"I won't tell him you gave it to me."

"And use it if you have to. Don't hesitate."

I swallow and feel the weight of the dagger as Michela slips out of the room.

10

CRISTINA

Once she's gone, I sit down, wincing, as I remember why everything hurts.

My wedding night.

What a hell of a wedding night.

The switchblade open, I set it in my palm. It's a little longer than my hand with an intricate handle carved from wood. The initials *M. D. S.* are engraved in the hilt. Michela Di Santo.

When I close it, it fits in my hand. I should be able to hide it in a pocket easily. As long as he doesn't search me, that is.

I get up to turn out the light in the room, take the bottle of whiskey, and sit back down, facing out the enormous window. I don't want anyone who might be outside to see me in here, so I need to keep the light out.

Liam is right. I need to be strong. I can't give up,

not if I want to survive. I can't let them break any other part of me.

I take a long sip from the bottle, having to force the burning liquid down. My fingers trace the pattern of the wooden hilt absently as I stare out into the dark night. I want to know what's out there in those woods. Both Damian and his brother know about whatever it is.

Did Damian know what would happen tonight? Did he know about the little welcome party? About the bloody sheet being shown to them all.

God, the humiliation.

And the little boy. Bennie? I glance back at the wrinkled, discarded drawing on the bed. I didn't even look at it really. How afraid must he have been tonight to see his uncles at each other's throats. To see me as I was.

Does he wonder about the skin of his mother's back? He's too young. He wouldn't know, not yet, but he will ask when he gets older. What will she tell him? That his uncle is responsible?

Did he whip her? That's the only way to get those lines, I think.

I need to be careful with him. If he'll do that to his own flesh and blood, what would he do to me?

I squeeze the knife in my hand.

Michela didn't need to tell me to use it if I had to. I won't hesitate.

I grin, drink, and listen to whiskey slosh in the

bottle as I remember that I've already stabbed Damian once. And his punishment was four spanks. He told me I was getting off easy, but four spanks compared to what I saw on Michela's back is more than easy.

And I realize something.

He won't hurt me like that. I don't know why I think that, but I do.

The wind rustles the trees outside. I stand, go to the window, and look down at the garden. There's a pool in the distance. It looks like it's been covered over for years. Somehow, I don't see this family lounging out by the pool on a hot summer day. I can't see them relaxing together at all.

The overgrown garden has not been maintained for a long while now. I can't see the path we took to the church from here, but the grass was overgrown there too.

My mind wanders to Edgar Allan Poe's *The Fall of the House of Usher*. How the house crumbled down around the family. How, as the family died off, so did the house.

I shudder, then take another drink. I drop the switchblade on the bed and walk to the closet to get dressed. I'm naked but for the robe and my hair is wet. I know I should stop with the whiskey when I stumble just as I reach the closet door. I haven't eaten since lunch.

I set the bottle down and switch on the light in

the closet. I look around at all the clothes. My clothes. He bought these things for me.

He has a weakness for you.

Does he?

I spy his sweater on the floor in the corner. I'd tossed it in there after he'd left it behind that first night. Or was it the second night? I can't even remember.

Picking it up, I bring it to my nose. It's soft. Cashmere wool blend. And it smells like him.

For reasons I can't understand, I slip off my robe and put his sweater on. It's huge on me, comes to the tops of my thighs, and I keep having to push the sleeves up. It feels good on, though. Comforting somehow. Like he's holding me.

I inhale deeply. I like his smell. I smell like him now.

Christ.

I shake my head because maybe I have a weakness for him, too.

Taking the bottle, I go back into the bedroom. I drink some more as I rummage through the drawer of underwear. He likes lace.

I pick a bright red string with a triangle of lace at the front. There's literally nothing to it. Setting the bottle down, I step into it, stumbling a little as I do, needing to catch myself on the dresser when I almost fall.

Does he like this? Me like this?

His.

I remember his mouth on me. I remember his body on top of mine. Heavy. Good.

I remember his cock inside me.

Am I a whore to want it again? Want him again? I should hate him.

Turning to the bed, I see the switchblade. I need to hide it. If he finds it, he'll take it away. He'll punish Michela again.

Her back. My God.

I'm crouched down beside the bed shoving the blade between the mattress and the box spring when a door opens. I look up to find Damian's eyes on me as he steps through the connecting door and leans against the wall, his damaged hand in his pocket. I wonder if that's just habit, hiding it.

I stand, my heart racing, and drop the covers back down. I must look guilty as sin from the way he looks at me. But then his gaze drops down, and I follow it and remember I'm wearing his sweater. Why did I do that?

Immediately, I start to pull at it to take it off, stumbling backward when it's halfway over my head so I can't see.

He chuckles.

"How much of this did you drink?" he asks as I try to get the sleeves off.

His hands are on me then, and he pulls the

sweater over my head, catching me when I almost fall.

He looks down at me.

I look down at me.

Naked but for the slip of a thong.

He grins, cups my ass and pulls me to him.

"I like that one."

I push at him. "Get away from me."

He does, eyes sweeping over me as he picks up the whiskey to drink some.

I drop to a seat on the edge of the bed and look him over as he spots my phone. He turns to me, holding the neck of the whiskey bottle in one hand.

"Did you go into my room and take that, too?"

"Well, it didn't grow legs and walk over here on its own."

"Don't do it again."

I lie back, suddenly so exhausted I can't sit up.

"I told you to eat. You can't drink this stuff on an empty stomach."

I look up at the pretty canopy over the bed, then at him as he comes to stand by my legs which are dangling off the bed. There's only one word I can use to describe the look in his eyes as his fingers caress my thigh. Lustful.

"Your sister's back," I say.

His face tightens, that lust gone. He drinks a sip from the whiskey, then sets the bottle down and looks me over.

"Don't worry about my sister's back."

"Did you really do that?"

His eyebrows furrow, and I realize my mistake. I get up on my elbows and look at him. I should fix it. He shouldn't know I talked to her.

"My father would only take her back if she agreed to two things. One was to change Bennie's name. She'd named him after his father. And rightfully so. But his name is now Benedict Di Santo. My father's name."

"Why did she agree?"

"Because she's weak. Get on your stomach."

I swallow. I know what he wants. I want it too.

He and I are weak too. Weak for each other.

But I push on. "The second thing was what you did to her?"

He studies me, then nods.

At least he doesn't lie.

I shudder, looking down at his hands. Big and powerful. Able to cause that kind of damage. That kind of pain.

"Are you afraid of me?"

I bite my lip. Am I? I was at first. I still am now, in a way.

"Will you really let me go?"

"I gave you my word. Now answer my question."

"Yes."

His face is rigid, body tense.

"And no. Am I being naïve to think you won't

hurt me like that, Damian?" I pause, then add, "You said truth in bed so tell me the truth whatever it is."

He relaxes a little. "You're stretching that *in bed* part."

"I answered your question. Answer mine."

"I won't hurt you like that. I shouldn't have hurt her like that."

I hear remorse in his words. I think about the dagger just underneath me, beneath this mattress. I think about Michela and about the evidence of what Damian is capable of, and I still believe him.

His eyes graze over me. That lust of earlier is a hunger now.

"Get on your stomach, Cristina."

My belly quivers, heat pulses between my legs, and my nipples harden. I watch him unbutton his shirt and pull it out of his pants. Lines of muscle cut across his belly.

I meet his eyes. They've gone dark. I roll onto my stomach, my elbows on the bed. I look at the closed door as I think about what he did the last time I was in this position. But this feels different. He's not angry.

He tugs the string of the panties. I shudder as he peels them down over my hips, my legs. Off my feet. I look back when he spreads my legs apart and stands between them. I watch him look at me, watch him crouch down behind me and open me.

I don't know what this is. I should pull away and

make him take it from me. But I want his eyes on me. And his hands on me. And his mouth on me. And him inside me.

"You are so fucking beautiful," he says, dipping his tongue between the wet lips of my pussy, licking the length of me before drawing back. "My beautiful little virgin."

I gasp and turn away when he puts his fingers on me and smears my arousal up toward my other hole, circling that too.

"And you're all mine."

Keeping one hand on me, he stands.

When I hear the buckle of his belt and the unzipping of his pants, I turn again.

His eyes are on my ass. He pushes his pants and briefs down, and I lick my lips. He's hard. And big. And my pussy clenches in anticipation even knowing it'll hurt. Knowing I'm still raw from earlier.

He rubs the whole of his hand over my wet pussy, then takes his dick in that hand, rubbing it, looking at me as he pumps his cock.

"Put your fingers on your clit."

I don't hesitate. I slide my hand between my legs, spreading my legs wider and rubbing my clit.

"Fuck." He watches, pumping his cock. "Don't come yet. I want to watch your fingers work."

He's tugging harder and watching him is making me wetter, so wet it's dripping down my thighs.

"Are you too sore to be fucked?" he finally asks.

My breathing is already shallow, and my pussy is greedy for him. I shake my head.

"I won't be gentle this time. I can't. And I don't want to hurt you."

I don't want him to be gentle.

"Tell me now, Cristina. Tell me to go or tell me to stay, but if I stay, I'm going to fuck you hard."

My hips buck at his words. I'm going to come soon. "Stay," I croak.

"Good girl." With that, he bends his knees as he lifts my hips a little. He's tall, and even though the bed is high, it's not high enough. Tilting my hips up, he pulls my cheeks apart and glides into me, my passage wet, lubricating his cock as he pushes slow and deep inside me, filling me up all the way. He groans, leaning over me, hands on the bed on either side of me as he holds still for a long minute.

"Your cunt is so fucking tight."

I rub my clit as he draws out and starts to fuck me just like he said, hard and fast and just on the edge of painful. It won't take long for me to come.

He moves one hand to my ass cheek, eyes almost black when he closes his thumb possessively over my asshole.

"You're beautiful like this," he says, voice hoarse. "Open and so fucking beautiful."

He shifts one hand, placing it over mine as I play with myself and all I hear are the wet sounds of our fucking, of our combined breath, of my whimpers.

"I'm going to come." My voice sounds breathy and I close my eyes. "Oh god, I'm going to come."

"Fuck," he draws the word out as I come, my walls throbbing around his cock, pulsing, milking him until he lets out a groan and stills inside me, gripping a handful of my hair in his fist. His entire body tense.

All I can think is how beautiful he is as I feel his cum inside me, feel him filling me up.

And as much as I know that Liam is right, that he has a weakness for me, I'm doubly sure I am as weak for him. In spite of everything, I am weak when it comes to Damian Di Santo.

11

DAMIAN

We're lying in her bed, Cristina still asleep. Her head is on my bicep, hands curled between us.

Last night when I walked in here and saw her wearing my sweater, I don't know what the hell I thought. I liked it, though.

After the debacle downstairs, I didn't know what to expect when I got up here. I know, though, that my sister paid her a visit from her question.

Sneaky Michela. What the hell are you up to?

Cristina mutters something, burrowing closer.

I look down at her.

She fell asleep before I finished cleaning her up last night. Passed out probably from the whiskey and the fucking.

The thought of that fucking stirs my dick.

She's perfect. Her body ready and wanting, her fingers eager to get herself off. Although maybe that's because she was drunk. Pretty sure, sober, she wouldn't so readily play with herself on my command.

But maybe she was trying to deflect my attention, too. It worked, if that was it. She was doing something when I walked in here. Crouched by the bed. I have no idea what, but she looked guilty as sin. I make a mental note to have a look around later.

I pull the blanket up over her shoulder. Her hair tickles my chin as she stirs, then sets her cheek against my chest with a quiet sigh.

I don't remember the last time I slept with a woman. Fucked, yes, but never slept with. Either I leave or they leave when I'm done with them. And I've never brought one home.

Not that Cristina would be here if she had the choice. I'm pretty sure she'd choose to be anywhere but here.

She's moving again, waking up slowly. Her brain is probably trying to process the foreign entity in her bed.

I grin. I'm looking forward to seeing her face when she sees me upon opening her eyes. When she remembers what we did. What she asked for.

I keep my hand on her hip. I can't fuck her this morning. I'm pretty sure she's raw after last night.

Maybe I'll get her off with my tongue before I let her out of bed.

As if on cue, her body tenses. I feel her eyelashes flutter against my skin as she blinks once, twice. Then seems to stop breathing altogether.

Here we go.

She bolts upright, wincing either from a sore pussy or a headache from the whiskey. Probably both. She looks at me accusingly, tugging the blankets to cover herself.

"Hey, don't be greedy," I say casually, tugging some of the blanket back.

"What the hell are you doing in here? In my bed?"'

I look at her, then let my gaze slide over her. One leg is free of the blankets, and it's like she realizes at that moment she's naked. I watch as the memories flood back, and I smile.

"There is no my bed or your bed anymore, sweetheart. There's only our bed. We're married, remember?"

"Get out!"

"Not what you were saying last night. Come here." I put a hand over her lap and make like I'm going to pull her to me.

"Get away from me!"

Sitting up, I lean toward her and brush her hair away from her face. "You invited me to stay last night. Don't you remember? You rolled onto your belly and spread those beautiful legs and begged me to fuck you."

Her face burns beet red. "I didn't beg you. I just... I was drunk. You took advantage."

"Do you remember how hard you came on my dick?"

She remembers and she's embarrassed so instead of answering me, she turns away. "What time is it?"

I check my watch. "Ten."

She looks over at me, down at the outline of my erection beneath the blanket, then quickly up at my face.

"Look, whatever happened last night, I was drunk, and it's done. We're not doing that again. There's no need. Your family even saw the sheets. Marriage is consummated. End of story."

"No, not the end of the story. We will definitely be doing it again. And what's more, you want to do it again. Don't lie to yourself, sweetheart." I push the blanket off and stand up fully naked.

Her gaze drops to my dick, which is hard, a state it is getting used to being around her.

"I'm not your sweetheart," she says, trying to avert her gaze.

"You can look. I don't mind."

"Well, I do."

"Come on. We'll take a shower, then go down to breakfast. I'm sure you're starving, and you'll want something for your headache."

"I don't have a headache, and I'm not showering with you or eating with you."

"You eat with me, or you don't eat."

"I hate you."

I turn to walk away. "Not what you were moaning—"

She throws the pillow at the back of my head.

I grin, picking it up as I turn back to her.

"I wish I had a rock to throw at you," she says.

"I'm going to pretend I didn't hear that." I toss the pillow back to her. She catches it, and I turn to go.

"Did you know that part?" she calls out before I get to the bathroom. "That they'd parade the sheets around?"

When I look back at her, I'm not grinning anymore. "It's not a big deal. It's done, and it'll keep you safe."

"So, you did."

"My family's traditions need to be honored."

"Just say you knew, Damian."

"I knew, Cristina."

"You could have warned me."

"And what would that have done?"

"What if I wasn't a virgin? What would you have done then?"

"Punished your uncle."

She looks confused. "What?"

"A part of the rules."

"I don't understand."

"He was responsible for you until I came to claim you. So those eight years your father bought, the burden of raising you and keeping you...intact... rested on your uncle's shoulders."

"Then why did you want to have that doctor check me?"

"Because I'm sure you had boyfriends he didn't know about."

She doesn't say anything.

"He got paid, of course."

"The apartment renovations and our lifestyle. That was all you?"

I nod.

"He did it for money?" Her face falls. "My own uncle betrayed me for money?"

"There was more. He wanted custody of his kids. I assured that."

"How?"

"I have some influence."

"They're with my aunt now, though. Simona is, at least, and Liam on weekends."

"Our agreement lasted until your eighteenth birthday."

She looks away, shaking her head. "This is crazy."

"Yeah, it is." I walk away then, into the bathroom, and switch on the shower. I take a piss while the water warms up, then step under the stream of hot water.

When I'm finished, I wrap a towel low around my hips and walk out into the bedroom. She's still sitting on the bed, but she's got a robe on and is hugging her knees to herself.

"Go get showered and ready. I'll wait for you."

"Are they all going to be down there?"

"Probably not. But you'll need to get used to being around them. I told you, you're safe now."

"How am I safe? I don't understand."

I sit on the edge of the bed and look at her. Even after the night she's had and hungover like she is, she's pretty. But she needs to eat. She's already lost a couple of pounds since being here.

"Did you hear what my father said to my brother?"

"That because of some rules he can't touch me."

"That's right. No one can. You belong to me. You're my wife. My property. Only I can touch you."

"What year is this? Did we go back in time, and I'm not aware?"

I adjust the robe at her breast, tugging it closed, tugging her closer. "It's what will keep you safe. Just like with those men at the party. They won't touch what's mine. If they do, they know there will be war."

"Your brother kissed me on the mouth."

My jaw tightens. "And he won't do it again."

"And all because you married me? Because I'm your *property*." Her eyebrows rise so high on her forehead they disappear behind her bangs.

"It's an issue of territory. We don't fuck with each other's territories and when it comes to my family, it's...tradition."

"So you married me for my own good." She says it mockingly, but she remembers my words from a few nights back.

"That's right."

"Should I thank you?"

I smile. "That'd be a good start. Should I show you how you can thank me?"

She smiles too, a wide, sarcastic thing. "If you mean by sucking your dick, you can be assured I will bite it off."

"Ouch. I thought you liked my dick."

"I wouldn't put my mouth near your dick."

"I wonder how hard you'll come when I put it in your ass."

Her mouth falls open, and I can't help but laugh outright at her expression.

"Fuck you, Damian!" She swings her legs over the bed and stalks toward the bathroom, slamming the door behind her. I'm still laughing when I hear her drag the chair that was in there, and I realize what she'd done with it. She must have it lodged under the doorknob since there's no lock on the door.

Good girl.

I get up, walk to the bathroom door. "So, does this mean you don't want me to wait on you for breakfast?"

"Go choke on your breakfast, prick!"

12

DAMIAN

Although I need her to eat, I'm too stubborn to send food up after telling her she won't eat unless she eats with me. Maybe I'll take her something later as a peace offering.

I'm sitting at the breakfast table with my second cup of coffee when Lucas comes strolling in. He pauses for a second when he sees me, making a point of looking around as if he thinks I've hidden Cristina somewhere, I guess.

Dickhead.

His hair's wet, but he hasn't shaved. There's a five o'clock shadow across his jaw on the undamaged side of his face.

"Where's your wife?" he asks, taking a seat and lifting the napkin onto his lap. From the table settings, I know Michela and Bennie have already eaten, but my father's place remains untouched.

Elise always sets the table like this even though my father hasn't eaten breakfast down here in years. I'm pretty sure Michela only does because of Bennie. She will have driven him to school two towns over where she'll pass the time shopping or sitting at a café for the few hours he attends kindergarten. She has never let any of the soldiers take him. Ever.

"She's not feeling up to seeing the family."

"I don't blame her after last night."

Studying him, I look more closely at what the plastic surgeons have been able to do. After the accident, almost the whole of one side of his face was burned away. Now, the damage is less, but he'll never look like he used to before the accident. Like me.

Strange to think of that. That this mirror image of me has changed so drastically.

"Get a good look?" he asks, lifting his gaze to mine. Elise pours him a cup of coffee when she enters.

She smiles at him. She's always favored him. I think it's because he's the one father had groomed to take over the business. Loyalty to the next generation so she wouldn't lose her position or some shit.

She tried to ingratiate herself to me when it became apparent I would be the one to take over, but I wasn't buying her bullshit. I don't forgive and I never forget.

Why do I keep her here now, though? So she

knows my hand is the one that feeds her. And it's the one that can choke her.

Not that she's worth the effort.

"How many surgeries have you had?" I ask him when she's gone.

"Lost track," he says, sipping his coffee.

"Why did you leave?" Lucas left the house after Annabel's death. I didn't realize he wasn't coming back until he didn't. And I can't put my finger on what I felt at his abrupt departure. I mean, it opened things up for me, but I didn't like it. Hell, maybe it was guilt at being in the driver's seat that night. Or guilt that what happened to him was so much worse than what happened to me.

What happened to everyone was so much worse than what happened to me.

Elise returns to place a plate of food in front of Lucas. He waits until she's gone to answer me.

"Why did I leave? I was only staying for Annabel."

Guilt again.

Fuck.

I look away, putting my cup down. I couldn't swallow if I tried.

"You break everything you touch," he says.

"I loved our sister."

"You still broke her."

Gritting my teeth, I shift my gaze back to his, making sure I mask any emotion.

"You're going to break her too." He gestures upstairs.

I don't breathe. I just listen to my heartbeat against my chest. Slow and steady. Under control.

"Unless she breaks you first," he adds with a grin.

"My wife is not your concern. Just make sure you stay away from her. You know the rules."

"I do," he says, his tone letting me know he won't be subject to them. "You want me to tell you I'll keep my hands to myself? Will that make you feel better?"

Bastard.

I choose not to engage.

"Now that you're home, you'll be going back to work for me." I shift conversation toward business. Those are the rules too. The family comes first. That means the family business. We all have to chip in and the days of Lucas getting a free ride because of that goddamned accident are over.

"And what would you have me do, Brother?" he asks, the distaste in his tone not so subtle.

"Keep an eye on the Clementi brothers. I don't trust them."

"Why not get rid of them?"

"I need you to manage them. Watch them closely. That's all."

"Is it because the old man was your godfather? Please don't tell me you've become so sentimental, Brother."

"They've been punished."

"Did it send enough of a message, though?"

"What would you have me do, kill them?"

"Just one of them."

I study my brother. "That's not what you would have suggested before."

"You don't know me like you think you do."

"If it's too much to ask, say the word, and I'll cut you loose. Out of the family business for good."

"You'd like that, wouldn't you?"

I shrug a shoulder.

"Like I said, you don't know me. You never did," he says.

"What's the matter? Are you pissed that while you were gone doing whatever the fuck it was you were doing I did the job you were supposed to do? And now that you're back, you want in? You want to take my place? Let me guess, you think I usurped your throne. But let me tell you something. I earned it."

"Let me ask you a question. How happy are you, Damian?"

I feel my face harden.

"Is taking your seat as head of the family everything you ever wanted? What do you rule over? A house of hate? What do you have? More money than you'll ever know what to do with?"

"Let me ask you one in return, Brother. Why have you returned if not to take back what should have been yours? What would have been yours had you stayed. Had you manned up and done what you were supposed to do."

I see his jaw tighten. His eyes narrow.

"Do you have everything you ever wanted in an unwilling bride?" he asks, continuing as if I haven't spoken. "I wonder if you'll repeat the cycle. If she'll birth twin boys. Brothers born holding hands who go through life with those same hands wrapped around each other's necks. And what happens to her then? You keep her like Dad kept Mom, knowing how unhappy she was?"

I drag a slow breath in through my nose.

"I'm curious. Did you do it to spite our father? Marrying the daughter of the man who destroyed our family instead of punishing her like you were meant to do?"

"I'm curious too, Lucas. Would you have punished her. Would you do to her what our father intended? You're not that cruel, are you? Although you never did stand up for those who couldn't defend themselves, did you?"

He knows exactly what I mean but he manages to keep his expression unchanged. Frozen. Like his heart. "You don't have feelings for her, do you, Damian? That's not what this is about, I hope. For your sake."

I push my chair back and get to my feet. "Keep an eye on the Clementi brothers. Anything goes wrong with the next shipment. I'm holding you responsible." I walk away and try to block out his chuckle.

"Take care, Brother. You don't want your enemies to learn your weakness."

I flip him off over my shoulder, not bothering to turn around.

13

CRISTINA

I'm starving and my head is pounding.

It's almost noon when I can't stand it anymore. I walk out of my room and go downstairs to find something to eat.

The dagger Michela gave me is in my pocket. I make my way silently down the hall and through the maze of corridors that I'm now learning. It's quiet in the main part of the house. I'm not sure where Damian is, but I need to eat something, and I need to get out of this room. Out of this house. Take a walk or something.

A fire burns in the fireplace of the foyer. They must always keep it going. Even with a modern heating system, I'm sure this house is too big and too old to heat without them especially in these bigger spaces with the vaulted ceilings.

The living and dining rooms are empty, the table cleared, and I don't hear a soul anywhere. I listen at the kitchen door, but it's silent, so I push it open, relieved when I find it empty. But even if someone were in here, they can't tell me I can't have something to eat. I live here now. They can't starve me.

On the counter is a basket stuffed with muffins and rolls. I take the biggest muffin I see, break off a piece, and put it in my mouth. It's good. Pumpkin.

I open the refrigerator to see what they have. Finding bottled water, I take two, tucking both under my arm, and then see a plate with the makings for a sandwich. I just need to find some bread.

I swallow the bite of muffin and close the refrigerator with my hands full. But when the door closes and I see who is standing just on the other side of it, I gasp, jumping in surprise. The bottles slip from under my arm and some of the things on the plate tip onto the floor.

Lucas catches the edge of the dish before it, too, goes crashing down.

The bite of muffin sticks in my throat as I stare back at Lucas Di Santo standing in the kitchen holding the plate of lunch meat and looking strangely amused.

"I..." I start but trail off. What am I supposed to say? I what?

He sets the plate down and bends to pick up the

food that fell off, tossing it into a trash can in the corner. He then picks up the bottles of water and holds them out to me.

"Take them," he says when I don't move.

I reach out, then remember the muffin in my hand. I've crushed it.

"Those are good," he says.

I just stare at him like an idiot.

"Let me guess," he starts, leaning against the wall and folding his arms across his chest. "My brother demands you eat with him, or you don't eat, is that right?"

"How do you know that?"

He shrugs a shoulder. "It seems like something Damian would do." He turns, opens a drawer and takes out a loaf of bread. "Here. It's fresh, baked this morning. Dishes are up there and utensils in this drawer."

When I still don't move, he raises an eyebrow.

"I don't bite, you know."

"But you do kiss."

He cocks an eyebrow. "I couldn't help myself. You're beautiful, of course, and honestly, I knew it would piss my brother off."

"You have a strange family."

"I agree. Make your sandwich." He gets a plate down for me and steps back, gesturing for me to go ahead.

I keep an eye on him as I set the remnants of my muffin on the plate and make a sandwich.

"Take your time. He's not here."

"I'm not worried about Damian."

"No?"

"No." It's a lie but I hold on to it. "Where is he then?"

"Meeting. My guess is he'll be back late in the afternoon."

"Is there some aspirin?"

He opens another cabinet, pushes a few things aside as he looks through it. He selects a bottle and holds it out to me. When I don't reach for it, his expression changes and at first, it's hard to read because it's not what I expect. Lucas looks almost resigned.

He puts the bottle on the counter, gives a small, sad smile then steps backward.

"Monsters most often don't look like monsters on the outside, you know."

I feel like a jerk.

I force myself to stand there and look at him. Really look at him. It's so strange, the beautiful side of his face, then the other side. He smiles at me and it's not monstrous. Not at all.

"I'm sorry," I say. "I'm not being very nice and you're trying to help me."

He shrugs a shoulder. "I'm used to it."

"That doesn't excuse it."

"Do you mind if I join you?" he asks, taking out another plate.

"That's fine."

He smiles again and gestures to the table. I take a seat and set one of the bottles of water in the spot across from mine. When he comes over with his sandwich, he twists the lid off, and hands it to me before doing the same with the second bottle and taking a sip.

"Eat," he says.

I pick up my sandwich and bite into it. He takes a bite of his.

"I'd just had a strange dream the other night, so when I walked into your room, I didn't know it was your room," I start, feeling like I need to explain. "With the music and the rain, and honestly everything that was happening, I was spooked. I guess I thought you were a ghost."

"I did come back like one. I'm sorry I scared you."

We eat in silence for a few minutes. It's awkward, but I don't know what to say. Every time I look up, I find him watching me. I can't tell if the feeling of unease is because of how he looks or just the way he's watching me. It's not right though. I have to remember that he can't help how he looks.

"Have you been gone a long time?" I finally ask.

He nods. "Since my little sister died."

"Annabel."

"That's right."

"That must have been awful."

"No more awful than what you experienced, I'm sure."

I don't know what to say. He's so different than I expected. So different than Damian. Compassionate.

"Can I ask you why you left?" I ask.

He points at his face. "This was worse, believe it or not. And I was in a lot of pain both physically and emotionally. When she passed away, there was no reason for me to stay."

"Why come back then?"

"Good question." He finishes the last of his sandwich, watching me so intently it makes the hairs on the back of my neck stand on end. Something flickers in his eyes. Something dark. That unease of moments ago is back, not that it had ever left, but now it makes my belly tighten. It's the feeling I had that first night in his room. It's gone as soon as it comes, but when he answers me, his tone is different. "You really want to know?"

"Yes," I say even though something tells me that no, I don't want to know.

But it's too late. The word is out. And his are on their way.

"To take back what my brother took from me."

A shiver runs along my spine. I hear the malice

in his words even though he says it with a smile on his face. A smile so much like Damian's but not.

"Don't you want to ask me what that means for you?"

I feel sick suddenly. Like the food in my belly has turned to rock. I put the rest of my sandwich down.

"No," I say, pushing my plate away.

"Are you finished?" he asks, gesturing to my sandwich.

I nod.

He reaches over and takes it, eating it greedily as he watches me, all teeth now. And all I want to do is run out of here. Run away from him.

I put my hand in my pocket, feeling the knife there. At least I have that. If he does anything, I'll stab him. I won't hesitate.

"Are you all right?" he asks when he's done eating my sandwich, that wickedness gone again like it's a switch he flips on or off at will.

I nod. I can't speak.

He pushes his chair back loudly, gets to his feet and rubs his belly, contented.

"Good. Don't worry, I won't tell my brother about our lunch." He winks like we're in on this thing together. "I'll see you later, Cristina." He says, walking to the door. He opens it to leave, but stops, and turns back to me. "One more thing. If he hurts you, you can always come to me. You have an ally in me."

I don't reply.

He walks out of the kitchen.

All I can think is how they all tell me they're my allies when I know in reality they're nothing but my enemies.

14

CRISTINA

After that disturbing lunch, I walk back up to my room a feeling of dread having replaced my hunger. I have nothing to do and spend the next few hours thinking, thinking, thinking. I can't concentrate on reading and when I try to call Liam, the phone goes right to voicemail. He's at school like a normal person. Like I should be.

I need to ask Damian for my laptop and internet access to continue my studies online. I don't see why he'd care either way. He's already given me access to the outside world with the phone, so if he's not here, it'll at least keep me busy. I wonder what he'd ask for in return. I remember our conversation this morning. About how I could thank him.

My belly quivers with the memory of last night even as my sex is still raw from it.

Movement outside the window catches my eye.

I scoot out of view as someone walks from the house toward the trees carrying something in each hand. From how he's bent, whatever he has must be heavy.

My heart races in anticipation of seeing Damian.

Except that it's not Damian. It only takes me a moment to realize it.

It's Lucas.

What is he doing? What is out there?

Without giving myself time to chicken out, I take my raincoat from the closet and put on a pair of boots. I don't have hiking shoes or even a pair of sneakers. I should ask for some. Tell him I want to go running or something.

Tucking my phone and knife into a pocket, I hurry out of my room. I'm careful to look out for others but not caring as much as I maybe should. I pass one woman vacuuming the living room. She ignores me as I hurry toward the back of the house.

There's noise coming from the kitchen, so I avoid it. But I notice a set of French doors off the dining room, so I head in that direction. I turn the lock and hurry out, closing the door quietly behind me. I follow a path in the grass that has been worn down.

Once I'm under the cover of trees, I know I can hide if he comes back.

I move as quietly as I can, but I'm not sure it's quiet enough as I crush leaves and break branches underfoot in the utter stillness around me. I hug the raincoat closer as a cold mist begins to fall.

The path becomes harder to make out as I creep deeper into the woods. I have to double back twice when I lose it altogether.

It's on that second time I see Lucas again. He's put his hood up and bent his head down. I don't think he sees me when I duck behind some bushes. He's going back to the house, no longer carrying what he had earlier.

I wait until he's out of sight before I move again, then walk in the direction he came. I'm almost sure I'm lost again when a path clears before me and the trees become less dense.

It's strange. I turn a circle and realize I can't see the house anymore. I'm not sure which way I came from after all those wrong turns. Suddenly I glimpse a two-story structure of some sort that is so overgrown it's almost been swallowed by the forest. I would have missed it but for the momentary clearing of clouds and the shiny glint of something bright. Like the sun reflecting off a mirror.

The hair on the back of my neck stands on end as I walk toward it. Is this where Lucas came? Where he left whatever he was carrying?

It'll be dark soon. I hesitate, afraid. Always afraid.

I should turn back and return when it's full light.

But I stop that line of thinking. I need to be

stronger than I have a been if I'm to survive this house of horrors. If I let fear stop me, I'm finished. I can't be afraid of the dark. I'm not a little girl anymore, and the games Damian and his family are playing aren't children's games.

So, I head in the direction of the structure thinking of Hansel and Gretel, thinking I should have left breadcrumbs. Wondering if a wicked witch is waiting for me inside.

I realize why the ground here is more worn down. At some point, it must have been covered in little stones. The trees around it must have been cut down long ago. Some new saplings are growing but aren't as old as the rest of the forest, so it's also a little brighter here even though it's a dark day.

After a few minutes, the structure comes into view.

Two stories, like I thought, and as large as a small house. It must have been a solarium, I think. All the walls are windows, the glass mostly gone now with only shards left here and there.

I stare up at it in awe. It's beautiful, or was once. Old, like it was built in the early 1900s with decorative curving arches. I can tell from what's left of the wood that it was painted white once.

Walking around it, I peer inside, seeing a garden table and two chairs, now green with moss. What I'm sure were once brightly colored tiles are now broken and litter the earth and it's as though the forest floor is growing into it. Reclaiming it.

Plants that must have been potted inside have broken out of their pots and now reach heights that, had there still been a roof, would have busted through it.

The double doors stand open. Well, the frames of the doors do. They, too, must have been glass. There are still shards of it here and there. I have to be careful as I make my way through them, picking up the faint scent of something floral and too familiar. Something left over from a different era.

Pins prick my skin, but I'm drawn deeper inside. My eye follows a beautiful, ornate staircase winding up to the second level. Some of the steps are rotted. The railing is intricately carved, magnificent and intertwined with thorny vines of a rosebush from which grow an abundance of deep red roses just past their prime.

It's their smell I recognize. Sweet and old like the roses he'd send me. Did they come from here? I always thought they came from the florist in the city but maybe not.

I look up from the roses and study the second floor, which is more a gangway that spans the entire solarium. The railing is wholly intact but for one place where it's mangled, the wood of the platform rotted away.

I stop to look at that for some reason. I don't

know why. But when a cold chill runs along my spine, I swear I feel eyes on me.

I turn a circle, searching the shadows. No one's here. I'm alone. But the thought doesn't comfort me.

Mist picks up into a steady rain. I need to go back. I *want* to go back. I never thought I'd say that. But something is telling me to get away from this place.

My heart beats faster and I find myself hurrying until I get to the table and chairs. There's an old teacup on the table. A child's tea set, I think. I walk toward it to have a closer look.

It's broken. Cracked in two, half lying on its side, the other half still sitting up in its pink saucer with the golden trim.

Not toys, actually. Too nice to be toys.

On the floor lie the remnants of a second cup and a small teapot. I bend down, wanting to pick them up but as soon as I do, I scream, falling backward on the ground because a pair of glass eyes is staring back at me.

My heart nearly explodes and I crab-crawl away, wincing as shards of glass cut into my palms. Even though I know it's just a doll, a very old doll imprisoned by weeds, I'm terrified.

Just a doll.

That's all.

A toy.

Like all those dolls in my room that night eight

years ago during the storm. The night countless eyes stared back at me.

I stop moving in order to look at my sliced hands. The bigger shards drop onto the broken tile, making a tinkling sound, like crystal. I look back at the doll.

She hasn't moved.

Of course she hasn't moved. God. I'm an idiot.

A little girl must have had a tea party here a long time ago. A very long time ago. That's all this is.

But then that feeling is back. Like someone's watching me. I shudder but force myself not to look at the doll as I get to my feet. I want to get out of here.

Blood smears my palms. It hurts, but there isn't anything I can do about it until I get back to the house.

I hurry out of the solarium as the rain picks up. Disoriented, I stop once I'm outside. Is this the entrance I used? No, the table was on the other side then, wasn't it? Is there more than one table?

Turning a circle, I see too many paths to choose from. Before I can panic, however, I decide on one, hoping it's the way I came.

I glance over my shoulder at the abandoned building. Why did I go in there? It's creepy, all of it. The broken railing. The china cracked and ruined. That doll forever alone in the dark, rain-soaked woods.

Shudder.

I hurry away. Night is falling fast. How long have I been out here? Clouds overhead hide the last of the waning light as rain falls heavier, plastering hair to my face. I realize now just how cold I am.

Tripping over rocks and tree roots, I try not to break into a run. I guess it was a ten-or fifteen-minute walk to get here from the house, but after walking for what seems like a lot longer than that, I realize I've been going in circles.

Because I'm back at the solarium. Back to where I'd started.

It takes all I have not to panic. Not to think there's something not right about this.

My hands throb with the glass embedded in them, and I know it's stupid, but I feel like something led me back here. Something old and eerie.

"Don't be ridiculous," I tell myself. Turning a circle, I look around, trying and failing to get my bearings. All I hear is the constant sound of the rain, and all I feel is the presence of that hulking, broken solarium with the doll trapped inside.

After looking left and right and back at the solarium, I start to walk. I just need to be away from here, but fifteen minutes later, when I'm again back in the same place, I can't stop the panic that takes hold of me.

I want to rub my face but remember the glass in my hands. I walk a few paces back the way I came but stop. I'll just end up walking the same circle again. I know it.

Pushing wet hair from my face with the back of my hand, I turn again, crossing to the other side of the solarium, giving it a wide berth as I do. When the cold wind whistles, I give in to that panic, hurrying my steps backward, keeping my eyes on the structure as if that would keep some monster from charging out of the place after me.

I trip. I'm not watching where I'm going. But I can't drag my eyes away from the solarium so when I crash into something hard behind me, all the tension I've been trying to keep tamped down bubbles up, releasing into a scream so loud, it sends birds I didn't know were even there noisily flying from the branches of the trees.

I bounce off whatever it was that was behind me almost falling to the ground until a strong pair of hands catches me.

I scream and scream until I hear him. Until he turns me, pulls me to him, and I feel his chest against my face and his hand cupping the back of my head and big, powerful arms holding me tight.

I scream until I know it's Damian.

Damian again, like last time.

Damian rescuing me from yet another ghost.

And those tears I'd almost managed to hold back pour out in relief even as I see the dark look in his eyes when he glances at the solarium, that haunted place.

He turns back to me and searches my face as if to know what I've seen.

Does he know about the doll? The broken railing?

Does he know the place is haunted? Because I have no doubt it is.

15

DAMIAN

I only found her because of the location device in her phone.

She's soaked through, hair plastered to her face, coat sticking to her, useless against the rain.

She shifts her gaze to her hands. I glance down at the broken skin, the smears of blood. But when I look back up at her face, I see fear. The panic of the little girl I remember.

I want to shake her. Ask her what the fuck she thinks she's doing out here in the woods, in the rain.

In that solarium.

But she's shivering, so when she glances back at the hulking skeleton of the once-beautiful structure with a strange look in her eyes, I wonder if there are ghosts here after all. If Cristina sees them and if Annabel still haunts what was once her favorite place to play. If I've been waiting for her in the wrong spot all this time.

This is where everything changed for her.

Where she became the cripple who couldn't crawl out of the burning car to save her life.

Guilt slashes my heart.

My fault.

Lucas is right. I break everything I touch.

I look at Cristina. At the sobbing, terrified girl she's become. Helpless. Helpless against us. Against me. Vulnerable. Breakable.

So much like Annabel.

You'll break her too.

He's right.

"We need to get out of this rain," I tell her as I hurry her along, catching her when she trips. I know these woods like the back of my hand, and I'm surprised that of all things, she found the solarium.

By the time we get to the work shed, rain is coming down hard. I decide to take shelter there and wait it out before going back to the house.

Cristina looks around as I fish my keys out of my pocket to unlock the padlock on the door. At least she's not crying anymore.

Her eyes fall on the tree stump with the ax sticking out of it. Wood that needs to be chopped lies in a jumble around it. Stacked against the wall of the shed is cut wood covered by a tarp.

"Firewood for the house," I tell her as I push the

door open and gesture for her to enter. We source it from the forest, and I chop it myself mostly. It's excellent stress relief.

Once inside, I light the lantern.

"Stay here."

I leave her looking around as I exit to collect dry logs. She's standing in the same spot when I return. She watches as I stack the wood in the stone fireplace and set about building a fire.

"Take off your wet things," I tell her as I ball up old pages of an old newspaper and stack them along with smaller branches for kindling before lighting it. I watch it take, blowing on it a little before wiping off my hands and straightening.

"I can't," she says as she tries to undo the buttons of her coat with trembling hands.

Going to her, I take her wrists to look at her bloody, cut hands, then back at her face. She's spooked. "You're all right. You're safe now, Cristina."

After a very long minute, she nods, but I'm not sure she believes it.

"What did you do?" I ask about her hands.

"I fell. There was a lot of glass."

I walk her closer to the fire and start to unbutton her raincoat. "What were you doing out there? How did you even find the solarium?"

"I..." Her teeth chatter. "I was following your brother."

"Lucas?"

"I saw him from my window."

"Lucas was at the solarium?"

"No. I don't know." She shakes her head, and I can't tell if the sudden shiver is from cold or fear. "Can we go to the house? I don't want to be out here."

"I've got you."

"I'm scared, Damian."

I take her shoulders and squeeze. She's not only scared. She's terrified. "I'm here. I'm not going to let anything happen to you."

Her forehead wrinkles, but her shoulders relax, and she finally nods.

"Now tell me where my brother went."

"I don't know where he went. I only saw him going into the woods then coming back out of them."

"He left you out there alone?"

"He never saw me."

"I doubt that."

She looks at me with a confused expression on her face.

I peel off her coat, taking care not to hurt her. Her shirt's wet, too, and her jeans. "You're soaked through. Do you know how long you've been out here?"

She shakes her head. "I couldn't find my way back."

"And that's why you won't go into the woods alone again."

"I don't ever want to go back there."

"Why? What happened? Apart from your fall."

Her forehead creases as she studies the fire. "It's just creepy. There was a doll, God, it was the scariest thing when I saw it."

"You got scared of a doll?"

She looks up at me. "It was old. Maybe an antique or something. When I'd bent to pick up the broken tea things, there it was, staring up at me from a tangle of weeds."

"Hmm."

"It was creepy, Damian. That whole place is creepy. I just…I felt like someone was watching me."

"No one was out there. We have soldiers, so no one would have gotten through."

But the way she looks at me, I know what she's thinking. Not a person. At least not a living one.

"You were going the wrong way, by the way," I say, moving off the topic of ghosts.

"How did you find me?"

I take the phone out of her coat pocket. "Location."

"Oh."

I'm about to set it aside when I feel something else inside the pocket. I take that out, too, momentarily confused when I see the switchblade.

When I turn to her, she looks from the knife up

to me like she'd forgotten it was there. And she looks guilty as sin. Like she did the other night.

I recognize it, of course. The intricately carved hilt. Pushing the button, I open it.

She jumps when I do.

I touch the blade—sharp as ever—and when I turn it to read the initials on the handle, I shake my head.

That's what my sister was up to that night.

I set both phone and knife on the mantel and turn to her.

She meets my gaze, shivering as rain taps on the tin roof.

"You'll explain that later. We need to get you warm and get that glass out first."

"It hurts."

"I can't clean them until you stop shivering so we need to warm you up."

She doesn't fight me as I take off her wet clothes. Only when she's in her underwear and bra does she seem to notice and try to wrap her arms around herself.

"Here. Sit down." I take off my coat and put it over her shoulders. I make her sit down on the chair closest to the fireplace before taking off her wet boots and socks. Her feet are freezing. She must have been outside for some time. If my brother saw her and left her to wander out there, I'm going to fucking kill him.

Grabbing the bottle of whiskey from the nearby bench, I bring it to her.

"Here."

"No, no more of that."

"Just a sip. It'll warm you up."

Bringing the bottle to her lips, I tilt it back so she can swallow a sip. I, on the other hand, take a big swig before setting it on the mantel.

After adjusting logs on the growing fire, I get the first-aid kit. She's lucky I've always kept a well-stocked one out here. Mom's rules when she was alive. I've just kept it up for some reason although I've never needed to use it.

"What is this place?" she asks. She's taking in the large space as I return to her. I wonder what she makes of the covered furniture along all the walls, only the few pieces I'm working on uncovered in this old, dusty shed.

"Work shed."

I drag a stool over, set the first-aid kit on the low table by the chair, and pull her hands into my lap.

"It's a little bigger than a shed," she says.

I shrug a shoulder and open the kit.

"Is this where you come when you go into the woods?"

I nod, finding the tweezers to pull out the glass.

"Ouch." She tries to tug her hand away when I remove the first shard, but I don't let her.

"It's going to hurt, but we have to get the glass

out. Maybe this will teach you not to go snooping since you clearly didn't learn your lesson the night you wandered into my brother's rooms."

"I wasn't snooping," she says as I get back to work. "I was just curious what your brother was carrying into the woods and where he was going."

The definition of snooping. But I don't comment. I'm curious too. "What was he carrying?"

"I don't know. He had something in each hand, like barrels or something. They were heavy I could see that much."

"You don't know where he went with them?"

"I didn't see. By the time I got out here, and after I backtracked to find the path twice, he was returning to the house. I think he was, at least. And he didn't have the things with him anymore. That's when I came across the solarium. How old is it, anyway?"

"Old. My father had it refurbished for my mother a long time ago, but it's been on the grounds since at least my great-grandfather was alive."

"Whose doll was that?"

"Annabel's," I say, keeping my eyes on my work.

"Your sister. Ouch!" I drop a small but sharp shard into the corner near the fireplace.

"Almost done."

It's quiet for a time. "Do you ever go there?" she asks.

I shake my head.

"When I was trying to go back to the house, I kept walking in circles, ending up back there. It was eerie."

I look at her. "Stay away from the solarium. Just stay out of the woods altogether."

"Did something happen in there?"

"Just stay away, okay?"

She nods and silence falls again, the only sound that of the rain on the roof and wood crackling in the fire.

"Is this your workplace? Do you make these things?"

"Used to be Lucas too, but now it's just me." I pick out more glass.

She surprises me when she turns her hand around to touch a rough spot in my palm. "I knew you did something with your hands." She circles it, and I watch her delicate hand inside mine. It's all I can do for a long minute until I drag my gaze to look at the top of her head, her attention on my hand.

"Lucas made that switchblade," I say.

She meets my eyes.

"Made one for each of us. I didn't realize my sister still had hers."

"When?

"When we were kids. Maybe twelve."

"You had those sharp blades at twelve? Why?"

I return my attention to picking out glass. "My father was never a gentle man. I guess Lucas thought he was doing his part to protect us." Does she hear the sarcasm in my voice?

She's quiet, and when I look at her, I find her eyes on me. "Did you make the doors at the house?"

"Yes," I say, picking out the last of the glass and getting to my feet.

"That's a lot of work."

I grab one of the bottles of water I keep out here and go back to her. "I like doing it. Gets me out of the house and out of my head."

"If you don't want to be here, why don't you just leave?"

I exhale and smile. "Things don't work that way with us." She studies me. "Hold out your hands."

"The Gates of Hell doors. They're appropriate, I guess."

She's got that right.

There's no running water, so she stretches her arms out in front of her. I wash the cuts as best as I can with the water before grabbing a towel and resuming my seat to dry them. I hold onto them, her hands closed in prayer, mine over hers in the same position around the towel.

"Did Michela give you the knife on our wedding night?"

She searches my eyes and gives a quick shake of her head. "I took it."

I cock my head to the side. "Really?" She's lying. "From where?"

"It hurts," she says, gesturing toward our hands.

I guess I'm squeezing a little too hard. I let up, set the towel aside, and get antibiotic solution from the kit.

"This'll sting."

She sucks in a breath but lets me apply it before I bandage both hands and close the kit.

"Thank you," she says, hugging my coat closer as I arrange her wet things near the fire to dry. She keeps her eyes on the fire. "For finding me. And for taking care of me."

"You're welcome."

A moment passes.

She shifts her gaze to the ground.

I grab another bottle of water and hand it to her while I drink straight from the bottle of whiskey.

"Are you warm enough?" I ask her.

"Warming up."

"So you took Michela's switchblade," I circle back.

She glances up at me then away and nods.

"Where did you find it?"

"I don't remember."

"No? I'd think you'd remember something like that."

"Can we drop it? You have it now."

"I don't like being lied to."

She turns her gaze to mine but struggles to hold it. "I'm not lying."

"I know you didn't take it, Cristina. What did she do, come to your room the night of the wedding while I was still downstairs? Were you trying to hide it when I walked in later?"

"She was only looking out for me."

I laugh outright at that. "Is that what she told you? If you believe her, then you're more naïve than I thought."

She plants her bare feet on the ground and stands, hands twisting around the bottle of water, my coat about to slip from her shoulders.

"I am not naïve. I'm trying to navigate this house of lies and liars."

I snort, take a drink, then let my gaze graze over her.

She notices and tugs the coat closer.

"I've not lied to you once, Cristina." Is that true though, I wonder?

"No? But you've kidnapped me. Taken my family from me. Forced me to marry you. And I don't believe that you haven't lied to me."

"I'm your ally in this house. Your only ally. Remember that. If you betray me, you have no one."

"Funny, I've heard that from all three of you now."

"Three?" She tripped up. I see the fact register on her face. "So when did my brother tell you that?"

"I meant two."

I set the whiskey down, then take her water and

put that aside too. I reach out to take the lapels of my coat and tug her close.

"You're going to tell me the truth, sweetheart."

She seals her lips and stares up at me. I walk her backward until we get to the worktable. I lift her off her feet and sit her on it. Her eyes grow wide as I study her.

After pushing the coat off her shoulders, I place my hands on her thighs and open them to stand between them.

She swallows.

I look at her mouth, then follow the jagged line of her scar down to her chest. I cup her breasts. Small but firm and round.

She puts her hands on my forearms but doesn't try to push me away as I reach into each cup and lift out her breasts, pushing the lace of the bra beneath each. I bow my head to run the scruff of my jaw over one nipple and watch it harden. The other I take between my teeth, and the moment I do, she calls out my name.

All the while, her hands remain on my forearms while I plant my hands on either side of her.

I straighten and smile down at her, seeing how her pupils have dilated. "Your eyes turn a deep violet when you're turned on."

She licks her lips, panting.

I reach my hand to her belly and slide it into her panties.

She sucks her lower lip in, hand tightening on my forearm but still not pulling it away or trying to push me off.

"You like this," I say.

Her breath comes ragged when I pinch her clit.

"You like me touching you."

"I…"

Drawing my hand out, I lift her a little, drag her panties off and tuck them into my pocket before pushing her back onto her elbows. Spreading her legs wide, I bend down and lick her slit.

She gasps, hands coming to the back of my head.

"You taste so damn good," I tell her as I circle my tongue around her clit and listen to her moan. And it takes everything I have to stop. "But you don't deserve pleasure right now."

She looks disappointed.

"No, you deserve the opposite of pleasure," I add, lifting her to stand, then turning her so she's facing away from me. I push her down over the table and drag her arms behind her to grip her wrists at her lower back.

"What are you doing?"

I slap her ass.

"Ow!"

I lean over her. "The knife. You ready to tell me?"

"Let it go, Damian. It doesn't matter."

I straighten. "Matters to me," I say, spanking her ass a few more times.

"Stop!"

"Tell me the truth or I'll use my belt."

"Belt?"

"Did Michela give you the knife? Think hard. If you lie to me, then you're betraying me, Cristina."

"What about *you* lying to *me*?"

"I haven't. Tell me."

"Is this some sort of loyalty test?"

I don't answer. Instead, I unbuckle my belt.

She looks back, eyes growing huge.

I watch her as I draw it out of its loops and double it over in my palm. I raise my eyebrows.

"Well?"

She looks from my face to my hand. I step backward and raise it.

"No. No. No. Wait!"

"Talk." I lower my arm.

She looks up at me. "You have to promise not to hurt her if I tell you."

I have to laugh at that. "Right now, right fucking now, you're worried I'm going to hurt *her*?"

Her gaze slips to my belt hand, then back to me. "Just promise. I'll tell you but please promise. She's scared, Damian."

At that I snort. "She's not scared, sweetheart. She's a manipulator." I raise my arm again.

"Promise!"

"I fucking promise." I don't really want to hurt

Cristina although I'd gladly wring my sister's neck for this latest betrayal.

"She gave it to me on our wedding night. To protect myself."

"Against me?"

She nods. "What you did to her…her back…"

"I've told you that I regret that. And if I could take it back, I would. I am not making an excuse, but you don't know the circumstances."

"You whipped her from the tops of her shoulder blades to her ankles. No circumstances would ever justify that, and you know it."

I bite the inside of my cheek as I exhale. "Yeah, I do."

"Let me up."

"Tell me about my brother. When did *he* tell you, he was your ally?"

"I went downstairs to eat something. I was hungry, my head hurt, and I didn't think anyone was there, but then he was in the kitchen, and he was… nice to me."

"Right."

"He sat down and ate a sandwich with me, and I don't know, we were talking. I can't remember."

I lean over her, angry with my brother as I squeeze her butt cheek, run the leather of the belt over it. "Try harder."

She nods. "Let me up. Let me up and I'll tell you."

I straighten, look at her ass. I like her like this. My cock likes her like this.

"Please, Damian."

Meeting her eyes, I relent and release her.

She turns to face me. We're so close she has to crane her neck to see me.

"I asked him why he came back, and he said to take back what you took from him."

"Well, at least he was honest."

"He looked at me strangely then, and I don't know, he wasn't nice anymore."

"Did he touch you?" My hand tightens around the belt buckle.

She shakes her head.

"What did he do?"

"He asked me if I was curious what that meant for me."

I grit my teeth. "And are you?"

"No."

"They're not your friends, neither Michela nor Lucas. You know that, don't you?"

"I know that I'm among enemies, yes."

If she means for it to cut me, it works. I don't show it, and I don't know why the words even have that power, but it does.

"He'll try to take you from me," I say.

"Does it matter what I want in this?"

"What do you want?"

"Does it matter?"

"It matters to me."

This obviously surprises her. I guess it surprises me too. "Why?"

I set the belt on the table and lift her to sit on the edge of it. I push her knees wide and stand between them. I tug her nearer. She's so close I smell her shampoo. Her skin. And all I want to do is kiss her. I think a part of me knows how fleeting this is. How easily it can all collapse around us.

I kiss her mouth, undoing my pants to take myself out before I lay her down, pulling her knees up so her wet cunt presses against my cock. I push into her and her muscles tense instantly around me. She's too tight, and I know it hurts her, but I can't help myself. I need this. Need her like this.

Will I always need her like this?

I give her a minute, licking my thumb and setting it on her clit, looking at her like this, my cock stuffed to the hilt inside her pussy, my thumb on her clit, her passage growing wet as I play with her.

"I love your tight little cunt, Cristina. I love how you get so wet when I touch you."

I lift her legs, set the backs of her knees over my shoulders and move inside her. She grunts with my thrusts. I kiss her cheek, her neck. I look at her as she takes my cock.

"It feels good," she says.

I draw back, just the tip of my cock inside her, punishing myself as I slide my fingers to her clit, rubbing just to watch her come undone. When I can't take anymore, I lean toward her a little, forcing her legs to bend more, opening her more to drive into her again.

She moans, eyes closing.

I slide the wet tip of my thumb to her asshole and press against it. Her eyes fly open, she's panting, and when I push into that tight little hole, she cries out. Her walls throb around my cock and I watch her come. Watch how fucking beautiful she is when she does, when she pants my name over and over, something I'm not sure she's aware she's doing.

"Damian. Damian. God. Damian."

"Don't betray me," I tell her, then straighten and push her legs wide. I look at her like this, spread open, my cock buried inside her. Her cunt wet and pink, walls still throbbing around me. Pressing her thighs to the table, I can't take my eyes from her face as I fuck her. I fuck her so hard that I force each breath from her.

I did lie to her once, I think as I'm in the final throes. And when ecstasy comes, when I release inside her, I realize I won't keep my promise to her. I can't.

Because I don't want to let her go.

Because I won't let her go.

16

CRISTINA

The smell from the fireplace is stronger than usual this morning, and I wonder if someone got overzealous starting one of the huge fires that warm the house. But when I get downstairs, I realize the fireplace is empty.

I inhale. Smell smoke.

"That was a mistake, Brother," I hear Lucas say from inside.

I slow my steps, listening as I approach the living room, when I see the soldier standing behind a pillar in the foyer. Actually, it's not him I see, but the end of his rifle.

I stop because it takes my brain a minute to process that it is a rifle. And when he walks out from behind the pillar to look at me, I realize it's an automatic.

Seeing them outside is alarming enough. But

having them inside the house takes it to a whole other level.

"Damian?" I ask, turning the corner to find him watching me from the dining room. He's standing with his arm on the mantel of the fireplace. Lucas is seated at the breakfast table and Tobias is looking out into the backyard. Two more armed soldiers stand inside the house by the French doors I used yesterday.

Lucas's dark gaze is on me as he picks up his mug and drinks from it.

Tobias glances at me, then at Damian.

Damian walks to the table and pulls out my chair.

"Morning," he says.

"What's going on?"

Last night after we'd come back to the house, Damian had sent me to my room. I'd had dinner alone upstairs because as soon as we'd returned, Tobias had required his attention. He'd looked even more serious than usual and Damian had been quick to send me away.

It wouldn't have taken a genius to figure out something was wrong. Very wrong.

After dinner, I'd fallen asleep before he'd come up. I know he didn't sleep in my bed, so when I looked into his room this morning, either the maid was very quick to make his bed, or he hadn't slept there last night either. Had he slept at all? I wonder as I look at him. He's changed clothes and his hair is wet from a shower, but I don't miss the shadows that darken his eyes.

I touch my pocket as I take my seat. He must have come into my room while I'd been sleeping, though, because I found the switchblade Michela had given me on the nightstand beside the bed when I'd woken up.

He didn't take it away. I thought for sure he would.

Unable to avoid Lucas's gaze any longer, I meet it. I can't read him at all. I'm getting to know Damian's moods, but Lucas is like a vault.

Did he really know I was out there when he walked by me in the woods?

"Sleep all right?" Damian asks.

"Fine. But what's going on?"

"Men are back. I'll go meet with them," Tobias tells Damian then walks away.

"Elise," Damian calls out, eyes on me. "Bring my wife some breakfast," he tells her. "What would you like?" I note the difference in tone when he speaks with me and it makes me think about what Liam said. That Damian feels something for me.

I'm too slow to answer, so Damian arches an eyebrow.

"Doesn't matter. Fruit and yogurt if you have it."

He nods to Elise, standing in the corner. She disappears into the kitchen while Damian pours me a cup of coffee. Then he sits down and looks at me.

"Michela and Bennie will be gone for a little while," he says.

"Gone?"

He nods.

"Where?"

"A camp out West. Something Bennie will enjoy."

"And Michela will not," Lucas adds.

Damian gives him an irritated glance, then turns to me. "How are your hands?"

"Fine. Still sore but not too bad. What's going on?"

"Nothing for you to worry about."

Lucas snorts.

"What the fuck is your problem?" Damian asks him.

Lucas glances at me, then back to Damian. "You should tell her the truth, that's my problem. She was out there yesterday." He pushes back his chair. "I'm going to hear what the soldiers have to say."

"Tobias will handle it."

"You trust him over blood."

"What choice have you given me?"

Lucas wipes his mouth, stands, then drops his napkin on the table.

"Just make sure you're ready to go. We leave within the hour," Damian tells him.

Lucas gives me a hard look, then leaves.

"What's he talking about?" I ask Damian. "And why do I smell smoke?"

Damian turns to me. "We had a security breach yesterday. Two men on the grounds."

"What?"

"Solarium is gone."

"Gone? What do you mean gone?"

Elise returns with a heaping bowl of fresh fruit, yogurt, and granola.

"Thank you, Elise. You can clean up later," Damian tells her, effectively dismissing her. He only continues once she's disappeared into the kitchen. "They burned it down."

"Who did and why?"

His jaw tightens, his eyes narrow, and I know he's distracted. He shifts his gaze to me. "Business," he says through clenched teeth. "Nothing for you to worry about."

"Nothing for me to worry about? I was out there. I felt like I was being watched. You think it was the men who set the fire watching me?"

He sips his coffee, licks his lips, and sets the mug down. He's pissed. I can see it. He looks at my plate. "Eat. I want to leave within the hour and I'm not leaving you here."

"Tell me, Damian. Tell me what's going on."

"I sent a message. Clementi sent one back."

"I don't understand. Who is Clementi?" As soon

as I say his name, though, I remember. The oldest client of my father's. One who doesn't want me around. I still remember his beady little eyes on me.

"Yeah, him," Damian says, pushing his chair back. "The asshole with the umbrella in his fucking drink." The look on his face is so dark, I think if he ever looked at me that way, I'd wither. He glances past me toward the front door momentarily. "What was Lucas carrying out there? What did you see?"

It takes me a minute to follow. "You think he helped them?"

"I didn't say that. I asked what you saw."

I try to think. "I'm not sure. I just know they were heavy from the way he was carrying them."

"If he betrayed me..." He trails off, schools his features. "You don't say a word to him, understand?"

"I wouldn't."

"Good." He checks his watch and pushes his chair back. "Pack a few things."

I nod just as Tobias and Lucas reenter the house. I can hear them arguing from here.

"Christ," Damian mutters, walking toward them.

"Damian?"

He stops and turns to me, but I can see he's impatient.

"Michela."

Coming back to the table, he lays his hand flat against the wood. I look at it, at his wedding band. I glance at mine.

He leans toward me. "I didn't punish her, if that's what you're going to ask. Didn't even mention it."

"Thank you."

"I sent them away for their own safety."

"What about your father?"

He grins, then straightens. "That old man will live to bury us all."

I shudder. "We're in danger." As stupid as it sounds, it's like the idea just dawns on me.

His expression grows darker. "I'll keep you safe. I won't let our enemies hurt you."

Our enemies.

Have I inherited his or have they been there all along and I've been oblivious?

I study him. He does the same to me. He cups the back of my head, as I turn my face up to his. When he leans down and kisses me, my heart skips a beat. I close my eyes and kiss him back.

When he draws back, his eyes are intense

"You're the only one I can trust right now. Don't disappoint me, Cristina."

Before I can reply, he's gone.

17

DAMIAN

The ride to Manhattan took a little over four hours because of an accident. I'm in the penthouse study with Lucas and I wish he'd shut the fuck up already.

"You shouldn't have destroyed it, Brother," Lucas says for the hundredth time.

"And I wouldn't have had to if you'd had your eye on the Clementi brothers like you were supposed to." I turn to Tobias. "Did we locate them?"

"Not yet."

"Aren't they married with kids?"

"Wives and kids claim not to know where they are. They're holed up with the old man."

"I want those two fuckers found."

After my warning to the Clementi brothers that I do not transport coke, they turned around and arranged for a fucking container of it to be shipped from Latin America to the US. The brothers disappeared when they were found out.

None of it sits well with me. It's not even so much that they tried again, but more so about how clumsily it was all done. How obviously.

I need to get my hands on them because there's more to this story than meets the eye. All I know for sure is I had the contents of that container destroyed.

The Clementis are out a lot of money, but they should have known better.

"Who has the most to gain?" Lucas asks.

I turn to him. He's leaning against the wall. I think about what Cristina saw. Could he have been carrying gasoline out to the solarium? Could he have somehow aided those men? Gotten them on the property to begin with? Would he?

He knows that forest like the back of his hand. We both do. And he can access the bunker as easily as I can.

The bunker was built by my great-grandfather. It's set in the rock of the mountain about two miles from the house. I'm pretty sure we'd survive a zombie apocalypse in there for more than a year the way it's stocked.

But it also gives us a way off the property.

Which, of course, leaves a way in.

I take a deep breath. "What were you doing out in the woods behind the house yesterday?"

"What?" Lucas asks.

"Cristina saw you."

His eyes narrow and he sucks his cheeks in as he calculates his reply. "Taking a fucking walk."

Well, at least he doesn't deny it. "In the rain?"

"I needed fresh air. What are you suggesting?"

"What were you carrying?"

"What the fuck are you talking about?"

"She said you were carrying something."

He pushes off the wall. "Let me ask you again. What are you suggesting, Brother?"

"If you had something to do with the fire, it won't matter that you're my brother."

"Business first with you, right?"

"I won't tolerate disloyalty."

"I'm not disloyal to my family."

"What were you carrying?"

"Gifts for Annabel and Mom."

That surprises me. The family plot is on the grounds just behind the chapel. I don't know why I'm surprised that Lucas would go out there.

"What kind of gifts?"

"A doll for Annabel and a tea set. She liked having tea parties. I'm sure you remember that."

"And what about Mom?"

"A plant."

"That's all?"

"That's all."

"She said they were heavy."

"Maybe she saw wrong. I had the things in bags, and I was hunched over against the rain. You can check to be sure I'm not lying. Have someone at the house go out to the plots."

"I will."

He shakes his head. "You're fucking unbelievable. You think I'd set a fire to destroy the solarium? The place Mom and Annabel loved so much?"

"I think you're too smart to set it yourself."

"You're fucking insane."

"Am I?"

"I'd think you'd have torn it down already, considering."

I grit my teeth.

Tobias's phone rings. He leaves the room.

"What happened to Annabel was an accident," I tell Lucas.

"A lot of accidents happen around you, Brother."

"The railing was loose. We couldn't have known."

"No, yet she's the one who fell. Not you."

"And if you think I don't wish it were the other way around to this day, then you don't know me." I stand.

"No, I don't know you, do I? I don't know what you're capable of, but I'm learning. Take Michela, for example. I've seen her back. You do that to her on our father's command?"

I look down, then back at him. "A mistake I will live with forever."

"What? You think that makes it okay? That you admit it was a mistake? You think she should forgive you?"

With a smile, I walk to meet him as he heads toward me. "No, I don't expect that. I know I don't deserve her forgiveness. But tell me something. If you'd been in my position, what would you have done? And before you answer, remember that I know what you're capable of. After all, I was on the receiving end."

He grits his teeth, looking away momentarily. "After all those years, you're going to wave that in my face again? Should I pity you? Beg your forgiveness?"

"Fuck your pity, and you already have my forgiveness. You always did. You just never wanted it. Is it because it's harder to live with then? Is it easier to blame me somehow?"

He snorts at that last thing.

"And yes, I am going to wave that in your face because you left. You fucking left, Lucas. After everything, after all those fucking years, you walked away."

"I had no choice after Annabel died."

"You always have a choice just like I always have a choice."

When he meets my eyes again, I see another side of him. The one from way back when we were kids. When we were friends.

"You know I never wanted any of it. That was our father," he says.

"You never stood up to help me, though, did you? Not even as I stood there and took it again and again and again. How many times did he beat you? I can count it on one hand. Me? Well, I don't need to remind you. And then what came after, what he made you do—"

"I tried—"

"You failed and I still forgave you!"

That glimpse of the boy is gone. Angry Lucas is back. "At least you were a fucking adult when I left. And besides, you've done well for yourself, haven't you? Got what you always wanted? So, don't go fucking blaming me."

"Why the hell are you back, anyway, after all these years? Why now?"

"Would you believe me if I told you I missed you, Brother?"

"No, I wouldn't. You're here to punish me for the accident that left you as you are."

"Another accident you walked away from. One in which you were behind the wheel."

"I tried to save you.'"

"Did you? Or was it your revenge for the years you think I stood by and let him beat you. Even when it was me he should have been beating? What about what happened after? What I did to you? You must hate me for that."

"That's your guilt talking, Brother. But hey, at least you admit it. You're wrong, though. I wouldn't hurt any of you."

"I don't know, Damian. I've had a lot of time to think about it, and you've always had a hard time letting go of a grudge."

"I have no grudge against you."

"Not anymore, maybe."

"That accident was Joseph Valentina's fault. He was fucking drunk. It was pouring rain. The roads were slippery, and it was dark. You know this as well as I do, for fuck's sake."

"All I know is I need a fucking drink."

I block his path. "You cornered Cristina in the kitchen."

He smiles. "She was happy for the company. I mean, what had you done for her? Abandon her in her room, not even feeding the poor girl unless she ate with you. Who the fuck do you think you are, anyway?"

"You scared her."

"Did I? I guess anyone would be scared of this, though." He turns his face a little so I see the damage more clearly.

I narrow my eyes but don't reply.

"Why so protective of her anyway? She's got a year, isn't that right? Isn't she doomed to the same fate as Annabel as soon as she turns nineteen? Slightly less than a year then, technically speaking.

You have to admit, it will be a poetic end. I'm surprised at Dad for thinking that up. Didn't know the bastard had any poetry in him."

"Shut the fuck up."

I turn away when he grins.

"Or won't you do it? At the end of the year? Will you betray your family and let the daughter of the man who killed your mother and sister live?"

"I thought you just said the accident was my fault. Or do the facts change as they suit you?"

"Tell me, will you betray us? Hell, maybe you're hoping dad will die so you won't have to go through with it."

"You don't know what the hell you're talking about."

"Don't I? I mean, why marry her?"

"So you don't lay your dirty fingers on her. I'm abiding by Di Santo family rules. No matter how enmeshed our relationships are, no matter how insane, this is the one thing that stands. You don't touch what's mine. And as my wife, she's mine."

"So, you did it to protect her from me."

"From you, from our father, and from her father's enemies."

"Well, that was very noble of you," he says sarcastically. "Selfless even."

"Fuck you, Brother."

"So you bought her a year? Doesn't make sense. Unless..."

"I said fuck you."

"There's more. You wouldn't do it if there wasn't something in it for you. You're hiding something, Damian."

I don't reply but shield my eyes as I study my brother because he knows me well. Better than I realized.

"Tell me something." He cocks his head to the side. "What happens to The Valentina Foundation if a terrible accident were to befall Cristina, and she should perish before her time?"

I keep my mouth shut. He's done his homework. He's not stupid.

"It would go to her uncle. To his line," he fills in.

"So?"

"So you'd lose control. You'd have no leverage."

"I controlled it through him while Cristina was a minor. It wouldn't be any different."

"But what reason would he have to continue with that sort of arrangement? I mean, I guess he did that in part to keep her alive."

"She was a child. There was no risk of not keeping her alive."

"But only because her father bought those precious years with his life. So, tell me, are you more devious than I thought?"

"You're getting involved in things that aren't your concern." Turning away, I pick up the bottle of whiskey on the corner of my desk and pour myself a glass.

"Just let me talk it out. See if I got it right. She's your wife. If she were to...say...get pregnant, well, then you'd be sitting pretty, wouldn't you? With or without her. I mean, after the baby comes and she makes you a daddy."

I tighten my grip on the glass.

"Humor me. Is that it? Is that your plan? To impregnate your unwilling bride?"

I face him, drink my drink, and study him. My brother. My twin. My enemy.

"She deserves to know, don't you think?"

"You don't care about her, Lucas. Don't pretend to."

"Oh, I'm not. But you do have me thinking."

"That's a first."

"And you know what I'm thinking? Brother?"

"I don't give a shit."

"You should because I'm thinking maybe that even if that is your plan, there's still something else. Something that hasn't quite gone how you expected."

"And what's that? Enlighten me."

"You've got feelings for her. All your plotting didn't account for that, did they?"

I grit my teeth and swallow hard.

"And you know what that makes her? A weakness. Have I found your weakness, Brother? Because if I have, then so will others."

Shooting out my arm, I grip him by the throat and walk him backward to the wall, my face an inch from his.

"You don't know me. You don't know anything about me. But I will tell you this. If you touch what's mine, I will fucking kill you. Are we fucking clear on that?"

His grin widens even as I choke him. "Does that mean I'm right?"

"Damian," Tobias says.

I don't know when he entered the room, so I don't know how much he heard.

"What?" I snap, not looking away from Lucas.

"We need to talk."

"You watch your back, Brother," I warn Lucas once more. "You said it yourself. A lot of accidents happen around me."

18

CRISTINA

I jump when the study door flies open, and Lucas storms out, rage darkening his features.

He stops when he sees me.

I remain frozen where I am in the kitchen, one hand on the tap, the other around a glass. I'd come in here to get some water when they'd started arguing in the study. And I admit that I stood riveted.

Snooping again, Damian would say. But I don't care. He married me to protect me. He told me that, didn't he? Does he truly believe this is for my own good? And is it for my own good or for some personal gain of his?

Lucas's eyes zero in on me, and he cocks his head to the side. "Get a good earful?"

I clear my throat and shake my head, turning on the tap and concentrating on filling my glass.

"No?" he asks, approaching.

I wait until the glass is all the way full before I look up at him again, using that time to try to school my features.

"No," I lie, sipping some water.

"Well, I'll tell you what." He walks toward me. "Is this your phone?"

I look at the phone I'd set on the counter. I'd just been texting Liam.

"Yeah."

He takes it, turns it around for me to enter my passcode which I'd set up the other night, then pushes a bunch of buttons before handing it back to me.

I take it.

"When you're ready to hear some truth, you call me, and I'll tell it to you. I know you may not believe this, but I am not your enemy, Cristina." He turns and walks to the door, grabbing his coat on his way out.

I exhale as soon as he's gone, but it's not a long reprieve because the door to the study opens again, and Damian and Tobias exit.

When they see me, they stop.

"I'll wait downstairs," Tobias says.

"Send Cash up," Damian says, approaching me. "How long have you been standing there?"

"I just came to get a glass of water." I sip from the glass.

He studies me. I guess he's trying to gauge how much I heard.

"I saw Lucas leave," I say, not wanting him to question me. He sees right through me if I lie. "He seemed upset."

"Upset is an understatement. I need to go. I'll be back late. Cash will be inside the penthouse. There are soldiers in the lobby and around the building. You'll be safe."

"Is it all right if I run a few errands?" I ask. "With Cash," I quickly add.

"What errands do you have to run?"

"I brought back a library book I should return," I say, and it's true. I did bring the library book with me that I'd had in my backpack the night he'd come for me.

He raises an eyebrow. "I'm sure the library won't miss your book."

"There's a café a couple of blocks away. I used to go all the time." I shrug a shoulder. "I miss my life, Damian." When he doesn't say no right away, I push on. "Cash can come with me. I don't mind. I'll just say hi to some friends."

He draws in a deep breath as he considers. "All right. Cash stays with you at all times."

"That's fine." He can be in the same café. It's a big place.

He nods, turns to go but comes back to me. He takes his wallet out of his pocket and hands me a wad of cash. "For coffee and whatever else you want."

Want. Not need.

I shake my head. I'm reading too much into it.

He's giving you money because he took yours, and you depend on him even for a stupid cup of coffee. How embarrassing.

"Thanks," I say, taking it.

His gaze sweeps over me and before I know it, he has one hand at the back of my head pulling me close. I'm not sure if he's going to kiss me or what but he brings his mouth to my ear and holds me like that for a moment.

"Be good, Cristina," he warns.

I nod, looking up at him as he draws back.

Cash enters and Damian leaves after giving him instructions to take me to the café. I pick up my phone. I scroll to where Lucas programmed his phone number, but I don't call it. Instead, I text Liam.

Me: Hey, you still at Roasters?

Although Liam had gone to stay with his mom initially, he's back with his dad until the end of the school year. I'm glad because it means I get to see him.

Liam: Yep

Me: Order me a latte. I'll see you there in a few minutes.

Liam: Did you finally grow a spine, Cousin?

He inserts a chicken emoji.

I send him the middle finger emoji.

"Ready?" I ask Cash as I put on my coat and slip the money into my pocket. There's at least several hundred dollars in there. I wonder how much Damian thinks coffee costs.

"After you," Cash says, opening the door.

Cash is exactly one step behind me for the entire walk. When I get to the café, Liam has a table for two near the window.

"Here," I tell Cash, handing him some money. "I'll be with my cousin. You go somewhere else."

"Mr. Di Santo said—"

"That you have to come with me, and you did. Look, that table just opened up. Grab it before someone else does." I walk toward Liam without waiting for him to answer me and drop into the empty leather armchair from which Liam removes his backpack.

"You snagged the good seats!"

"Sure did. It's good to see you out and about," Liam says and hands me a large cup.

I take it, wrapping my hands around the warmth of it. "It's good to be out and about," I say, truly smiling and meaning what I say. I didn't realize how much I missed the city. The busy streets. Even the never-ending sound of horns honking.

"How are things? How are Simona and your mom?"

"They're doing all right. Simona misses you."

"And Uncle Adam?"

His face grows darker. "He's drinking."

"He was always drinking."

"No, not like that. It's bad now. I don't know what's going on in his head. I hope it's that he feels like an asshole for what's happening to you."

"He shouldn't. He couldn't have stopped Damian."

"What happened to your hands?"

"Oh. I fell."

He raises his eyebrows. "You fell? Or did he hurt you?"

"He?" I'm confused for a moment but then I realize he means Damian. "No, Damian doesn't hurt me."

From the look on his face, I'm not sure he believes me.

"I mean it. I fell into broken glass. He picked it out, actually. And bandaged me up."

"If he raises a hand to you—"

"He won't. I promise. He's not like that." It's strange, saying this to Liam, but it's true. When it comes to me, at least.

"Those goons with you?" Liam asks, sipping from his cup as he gestures with his eyes at the two men standing across the street.

"I think only that goon is with me," I say, nodding my head toward Cash although the men across the street seem goonish enough to work for Damian.

"So, I learned some interesting things you might want to know about."

"Yeah?"

Liam reaches into his backpack and extracts his laptop but doesn't open it yet. He just sets it on his lap.

"Did you know Annabel was paralyzed from the waist down?"

"No. I had no idea."

"I found some hospital records," he starts, opening his laptop and turning it toward me as he looks behind us. Liam has a talent for finding things online most people don't have access to. I guess he's an amateur hacker. I don't know everything he's done, he's pretty secretive about it, but I do know he's been able to hack into his high school's system to change a grade or two. I have a feeling that's the most innocent thing on his resume.

"How?"

He shrugs a shoulder. "I'll give you the gist of it. She was just a normal kid until she was about six. Homeschooled and no friends and shit, but otherwise as normal as you can be growing up in that family. But she was hospitalized for some time after a bad fall."

"A fall?" My mind immediately moves to the broken railing in the solarium.

"She broke her back."

I scroll through the records, look at photos, pick up bits and pieces of text although most of it is written in lingo I don't understand since I'm not a doctor.

"Do you know where the fall took place?"

He takes the laptop back, and I follow his finger strokes as he toggles between screens.

"Solarium."

He turns it back to me, and I swallow. It's the solarium where I'd been just yesterday, where I'd felt like I was being watched. Where I'd seen that doll.

I shudder.

"Police report," Liam adds on. "I guess one of the maids had called it in since the parents weren't around, and when the ambulance came, so did the cops."

It looks very different to the overgrown broken glass house I was in yesterday. Well maintained. I can almost imagine how it must have smelled with all the roses blooming up along the staircase.

"She was playing in the solarium with Damian at the time of the accident."

"What?"

"He was a couple of years older than her. I guess it's nice he played with her."

"Was anyone else with them?" I ask, remembering what I overheard in the study this morning. The comment Lucas made about accidents happening around Damian. The mention of Annabel.

"Not according to the report. They were the only two home along with the maid. Elise or someone."

"Elise is still there." I look at the photo of Elise as a younger woman. I wonder if she was a bitch back then too. She looks like one.

"That's where she fell from?" I point to the place.

"Looks like the railing was loose."

"It's still loose. Or it was," I tell him as I close the lid of the laptop. "Actually, the solarium is gone now."

"What do you mean?"

"Someone burned it down. Arson."

"What?"

"That's why we're here. That place is like a fortress, but someone got in and set fire to the solarium. I have no idea why they'd choose that building instead of the house. Damian said it was to send a message."

"Who sent a message?"

"A man named Clementi. He had some work with Dad too, according to Damian."

"Clementi." He jots the name down on the palm of his hand. "Someone got on the grounds of the Di Santo house?"

I nod.

"It has to be an inside job. Found this aerial image, too." He flips to another photo, and I see a vague image of the house and the grounds taken from a drone maybe. It's not quite clear, but I can see how secure it is with the mountain and forest, the tall stone fencing where there isn't a natural barrier and, of course, the guard tower.

"Damian thought Lucas might be involved," I say with a lowered voice after I glance at Cash to make sure he's not listening. The café is loud, though, and he's far enough away.

"What do you think?"

"I'm not sure. I don't like Lucas, but I mean, they're brothers. Twins. Would he really do that to his own family?"

"Well, I have one more thing you should see." He takes the laptop back and punches a bunch of keys before turning it back toward me.

I read what's on the screen. "What's this?" I ask, recognizing the address of my old house on Staten Island.

"The house was sold almost immediately after your father's death."

"I know."

It was weird, considering the alleged suicide. The real estate agent said it would be a hard sell, but it wasn't. After hearing that it had sold, I didn't give it much thought. I didn't want to. There were too many painful memories that I was okay to leave alone.

"Don't you want to know who bought it?"

"This corporation?" I point at the name on the screen. "I don't know why a corporation—"

"Shell company. If you peel back the layers, guess who technically owns your old house."

"Who?"

"Guess."

"Just tell me, Liam."

"Your husband."

19

CRISTINA

"He doesn't act like a man who just lost twenty million dollars," Damian says to Tobias as he walks into the penthouse.

Sitting up, I rub my face and look over at him. He looks fierce, angry. And like he's had a long day. The clock on the wall tells me it's almost midnight.

"I'll be down in a few minutes," he tells Tobias who nods and leaves again. When he reaches the couch, he takes the remote and switches off the TV. "Why didn't you go to bed?"

"I just dozed off. I need to talk to you."

"It's not a good time." He checks his phone after it dings with a message, running a hand through his hair as he reads it, his attention wholly absorbed by it.

"It's not a good time for me to be cooped up in here on my own most of the day either."

He texts his response then gives me a sideways glance as he takes off his coat, tosses it over the back of the couch and heads toward his study "It's been a long day. Go to bed. We can talk tomorrow."

"Why did you bring me if I was just going to be in your way?"

"You're not in my way."

"Well, all you've done since we got here is send me away."

He stops, turns to me. "What? Do you suddenly miss me? You want to spend time with me? That's not the impression you've given me so far, sweetheart. Go to bed."

"I have questions."

"Christ. Look, it's been a really long day and it's not over yet. Can it wait until tomorrow? I'm just up here to grab some things and go."

"Go where?"

"Business."

Vague as ever. Who does business at this time of night? I follow him into the study.

"Who doesn't act like a man who lost twenty million dollars?" I ask, not yet ready to ask the real question.

"Don't worry about it."

"Why do you keep telling me not to worry about things but expect me to understand that I need to be accompanied by your soldier?"

"This is business, Cristina. You won't be involved

in that. All you need to know is that I'll keep you safe." He opens a couple of drawers and fishes through until he finds what he needs. He tucks the papers into his jacket pocket and looks at me with both eyebrows raised.

"Why were you and your brother fighting today?" I ask.

"Brothers fight. This is what couldn't wait?"

"I heard my name."

"Were you snooping? Listening at the door? When will you learn your lesson?"

"I was getting a glass of water and you two were loud."

He surveys me. "We were born holding hands. Did I ever tell you that?"

"You rarely tell me anything."

"I tell you what you need to know. And besides, this situation, you and me, it's gone a little differently than I expected." He checks his watch. "I have to go. We'll talk tomorrow."

"Differently how?"

He shifts his attention to his phone when another message comes through. "Nothing. Never mind."

"See? This is an example of how you don't tell me anything."

"Cristina." The way he says my name is with a groan of irritation.

"I mean it. You—"

"How is your cousin?" he asks with a smirk.

I guess he's making a point. I'm surprised he knows, although I shouldn't be. I'm sure Cash reports everything back to him. "Fine."

"Why didn't you mention you'd wanted to see him?"

"I ran into him. That's all."

He touches a knuckle under my chin and tilts my face up. "You know how I can tell when you're lying?"

I turn my face away.

"That's it exactly. You can't hold my gaze. Now are you done? I need to go."

"Where?"

"This again?"

He attempts to walk past me, but I grab hold of his arm. Not that I can stop him if he wants to go but he does stop, looks at my hand then at me.

His phone dings with yet another message but he ignores it this time, turning his full attention to me and I'm suddenly not sure I want it. He walks me backward to the desk, placing his hands on it on either side of me when the backs of my legs hit it.

"What's the matter, sweetheart? You need some attention? I'll tell you what. I can spare a few minutes." His gaze drops to my lips and I realize I'm licking them. "Bend over the desk."

"What?"

"Bend over, lift your skirt and I'll take care of you before I go."

"That's not...You're a jerk, you know that?" I try to slip past him, but he captures my arm to stop me, ignoring another message notification.

"You wanted me. You have me."

"Not like this."

"This is what you get. You had a question."

"You're in no mood to answer it." I squirm but there's no getting away from him.

"No, I'm not, because like I said it's been a really long fucking day. So why don't you bend over the desk and at least make yourself useful." He spins me around, swipes his arm across his desk to clear it, sending all the papers on top to the floor before pushing me down over it.

"Is this why you brought me? To make myself useful when you have *long fucking days*?" I say, looking back at him as he pushes the skirt of my dress up to my waist and my panties down over my hips.

I attempt to push the skirt back down.

"It's one of the reasons."

I hear another message notification and again, he ignores it. He captures my wrists, holding both in one hand at my lower back and lifting my skirt again.

He undoes his belt, his pants and I shouldn't be fucking turned on, not like this, but I am.

"Besides," he starts, lining up his cock at my entrance and keeping eye contact. "I like having you around."

He slides his length into me and as much as I don't want to want this, I'm wet.

"Fuck," he groans, drawing the word out.

"This isn't—" I start to protest but he pulls back and thrusts in, forcing the air from my lungs.

"Don't worry, I'll make you come even though I shouldn't."

"How generous..." he slips a hand between my legs and I lose my train of thought, gasping with the contact.

"Don't be a smartass. You want this as much as I do."

I should to tell him to piss off, make him answer my questions but when he touches me like this I can't think straight.

He thrusts again, fingers playing with me, fucking me harder than he has before. I bite my lip so as not to cry out as the sounds of our fucking, wet and lewd, fill the room.

"After I fuck this tight little cunt you're going to get on your knees and clean my dick. What do you think about that, sweetheart?"

"I hate you."

He leans over me and I feel sweat drip from his forehead onto my temple. He kisses my cheek, licks the shell of my ear. "It's a good thing I don't hate you, isn't it?"

I don't answer. I guess I'm surprised by it.

"Come, Cristina." He's breathing hard, fucking me harder, beads of sweat on his forehead as he straightens again. "Let me feel you come on my dick."

I don't want to come. I don't want to want him or be turned on by him but god when he moves like this inside me and works his fingers over my clit, when I see his eyes darken, see the want inside them, I can't help it.

I come.

And when I do, I feel him thicken inside me and he thrusts twice more then stills, a moan coming from deep inside his chest, eyes closed, ecstasy on his face as his cock throbs and he fills me up.

We're both panting when he opens his eyes finally and meets mine.

"You are so bad for me," he mutters, pulling out of me, cum sliding onto my inner thighs as he does. He looks down at my ass, keeping me bent over for a minute before turning me to face him. He cups my head with one hand, his other hand on my arm, eyes dark and intent. "So fucking bad."

Pulling me toward him, he kisses me hard before roughly breaking away to lower me to my knees.

"What are you doing?"

"You mean what are you doing. You're going to clean my dick, sweetheart."

"What?"

He makes a fist of my hair and painfully forces me to look up at him. "Don't bite."

20

CRISTINA

I'm not sure I've ever felt more humiliated.

Or more aroused.

I hate myself for that last part.

After using my mouth to clean his dick, he gave me a long look, put himself back in his pants, and turned and walked out of the door and out of the penthouse.

Asshole.

And the worst part? I came. I came on his command and we both know it.

I'm not sure what's wrong with me. Not sure who I am when it comes to him.

It's late morning and I'm just wrapping up my shower. He's gone again. I'm not even sure he slept last night. If he did, it wasn't in the same bed as me, and as much as I don't want to care, that bothers me.

I'd waited up to talk to him. To ask him why he

owns my house. Because it makes no sense to me. I mean, is he even using it? Is it collecting dust? Isn't it macabre to want to own the house where you hanged a man?

It's just weird and creepy.

Lucas's words repeat for the hundredth time in my ears. *When you're ready to hear some truth, you call me, and I'll tell it to you.*

Back in the bedroom, I pick up my phone from the nightstand to read the number Lucas programmed into my phone. Can I trust him to tell me the truth? Or will he twist everything? Tell me lies and half-truths that will only confuse me more than I already am? But I don't have many options. Last night showed me exactly where I stand.

And I need to get some answers.

Sitting on the edge of the bed, I push the call button.

Lucas answers on the third ring. "Cristina."

Something cold snakes along my spine at the way he says my name, like he's been expecting me to call. Like he's known all along I would. It makes me want to run and hide. But I steel my spine.

I've been hiding for too long.

"Did you mean what you said?" I ask, my voice coming out more forceful than I intend.

He chuckles.

"Did you? Are you going to tell me the truth?"

"Are you ready to hear it? If you're calling me, it means my brother isn't being forthcoming."

"I don't trust you."

"That's good. You shouldn't trust me or anyone else."

"What the fuck, Lucas?"

"Where are you?"

"At the penthouse."

"Can you get to the café you went to yesterday?"

"How did you know about that?'

"Can you?"

"I think so."

"I'll meet you there in twenty minutes."

"Wait," I say before he hangs up.

"Yes?"

"Can you just tell me on the phone?"

"Are you afraid of my brother finding out you saw me? Or is it that you're afraid of me?"

"I'm not afraid of either of you," I lie.

He snorts.

"If you're just going to play games with me too, then forget it."

"Café. Twenty minutes. If you're there, I'll know you're serious." With that, he disconnects.

I take a deep breath in and get up to get dressed. I towel dry my hair, and walk into the living room to find Cash standing at the door, exactly where I expect him.

The woman who made my breakfast the other

day and my dinner the night before is in the kitchen washing dishes.

After greeting her, I pick up my coat and walk right up to Cash. I'm not sure he's going to let me go. Not sure if Damian has forbidden it or something after last night. But before I can say anything, he opens the front door.

"Same café?" he asks.

Confused, I nod but go along, not wanting to screw up my chance.

Lucas isn't there when we arrive, and I wonder if I'm too late or if he won't show. I order a cappuccino, just picking it up, when I feel the cool breeze of the door opening. I don't have to turn around to know it's him. That same sensation—icy fingers along my spine—are enough to tell me.

I take my coffee, thank the barista and turn to find Lucas's eyes on me.

He's tall, as tall as Damian, and has a presence that, like Damian, makes people sit up and take notice.

Or maybe that's his face.

In a strange way, there's a part of me that feels sorry for him. I don't know what it is. Maybe it's just because of what happened to him. What he has to live with. The people staring in the café is just one example.

But I shake my head because I need to remind

myself that he's ugly on the inside, too. It'd be outright stupid to let myself forget that.

He shifts his gaze to Cash, and I do too, expecting interference. But the two just nod to each other. Lucas opens the door and gestures for me to exit.

I look at the waiting car with the black tinted windows.

I look back at Lucas.

My heart hammers as I walk toward him. I hope I give the impression of being a little more confident than I feel.

"You said you'd meet me here. I'm not going anywhere with you."

"I'm not going to hurt you, Cristina. I'm taking a risk too."

"Why can't we just talk here?"

"Because I'm not alone."

He turns to the car. I follow his gaze to the passenger side window. It slides halfway down and sitting inside is, of all people, my uncle.

21

DAMIAN

"Is everything ready?"

"Just waiting on your call."

"Good. Let's go."

I climb into the SUV and we head to the restaurant where I'll meet Arthur Clementi at his request. The old man claims to have information for me. If it's what I think it is, he will have bought leniency for his sons. I wonder if my dad would do for me what he's doing for his boys.

No, no need to wonder.

I know that answer.

The restaurant is about an hour out of town. Only three other cars occupy spaces in the parking lot. It's closed this time of day and when I walk inside, I find the dining room empty but for the table in the back where Arthur is seated. At a quick count,

I see he has the agreed upon number of men who are standing not so discreetly around the room.

He's scared.

That's good.

Tobias and his men fan out and Clementi stands.

"Arthur," I say in greeting once I reach the table. He's aged since I last saw him and now looks every bit his seventy-five years.

"Damian."

He extends his hand. This is good. I take it, gripping it firmly.

"Thank you for coming," he says.

"The men who set the fire are dead," I tell him. He turned them over himself. Men who worked for his sons. A gesture of goodwill, or so he called it.

"Short life spans in our business," he says casually.

"Not for all of us, I hope." I wonder if the soldiers working for him know how easily they will be sacrificed if it comes to that.

"Listen, Damian, my boys—"

"Are not boys but men."

"They made a mistake. I—"

"I assume I'm here because you have information you believe I'll want?"

I had a gut feeling about the contents of that container not belonging to the Clementi family. I'd been right. Arthur has left the running of the business to his sons for just over a year now. They've managed to fuck it up royally.

Of course, that's my opinion, but I can tell you after this, they'll be out of business. In fact, they'll be lucky to walk away at all. Well, hobble away.

In this case, his sons had made the arrangements without their father's knowledge. When things went south, they asked him to lie and told him it was life or death. And it will be if the information Arthur gathered doesn't line up with what I'm thinking. Just not old man Clementi's life. I'll take one of his boys. They can decide which one between them.

I remember Lucas suggesting the same thing just a few days ago, but if Clementi confirms my suspicion then I have bigger fish to fry.

Clementi raises a finger, and one of the men—I guess his attorney because he's definitely not the muscle—steps forward and produces a folder.

"Thank you," Clementi says, and the man steps away. He passes the folder to me, and I open it.

"Cash trail. Your enemy is much closer to home than me or my family, Damian. My sons were used."

"Your sons let themselves be used," I say as I leaf through the pages. I've known about my enemies being close to home for a long time. This just confirms it. "I appreciate you being up front with me, Arthur." I close the folder and stand.

He reaches out to place his age-spotted hand

over mine. "I gave you the information. I condemn what they did. Let me punish them. My sons—"

"I will punish your sons, but their lives will be spared. I gave you my word and you know I'm good for it."

I hope he won't stoop to begging. My answer won't change, and he'll only humiliate himself.

He nods his head. "I trust your word. Thank you, Damian."

I gesture to Tobias. A moment later, I'm back in the SUV.

"Where's my brother?"

22

CRISTINA

I meet my uncle's eyes as soon as I'm on the sidewalk. "Uncle Adam?"

"We should get off the street before anyone sees us together. Get in the car. It's safe," my uncle says.

I turn from him to Lucas and back. "With him?"

He nods.

"Are you sure?"

"Please, Cristina. We don't have much time."

Lucas opens the back door and after a moment's hesitation, I climb in. Although I'm not sure it is safe because I'm not sure I trust my uncle. But I need to hear what Lucas has to say.

As soon as he closes the door, I lean toward the front seat. "What's going on? Why are you here with him?"

"We'll talk soon," he says, half-turning his head,

the look on his face worried. I notice he has a few more grays around his temples and the line between his eyebrows seems to have deepened.

I watch Lucas walk around the car to the driver's side door. Cars honk their horns at us. Lucas is double parked, blocking traffic and from the look on his face, he couldn't care less. He gives the man in the car behind us the finger, then climbs into the driver's seat, starts the engine, and pulls away from the curb.

I look over my shoulder into the café. "Is Cash going to follow us?" I can still see my bodyguard sitting in the same place, sipping his cup of coffee.

"No, why? Is that going to be a problem? If you need a babysitter, we have your uncle. He's a real joy to be around."

"Well, he's supposed to stay with me. Damian said—"

"I doubt Damian knows you called me so I wouldn't worry about what he has to say."

"So, he's just going to let you take me?"

He glances back at me. "Don't be dramatic. I didn't exactly take you. You walked out of that café and into my car of your own free will."

"Won't Damian find out?"

"You weren't going to tell him? You seem to tell him everything else."

"That's not true."

"Isn't it?"

I look out onto busy Manhattan traffic. "Where are we going?"

"Your uncle's place."

I'm surprised, but I guess it makes sense. No one to see us or overhear us there. Liam will still be in school and there's no one but the maid.

It's a twenty-minute ride, Lucas parks his car in the garage beneath the building, and he and my uncle both climb out when we get there. I can hear how hard my heart is racing when I'm alone in the car. My hands, still clasped around my coffee cup, feel clammy as I unclasp them when Lucas opens my door.

"Are you coming?"

I put my untouched coffee in the cup holder and undo my seat belt to climb out, ignoring his proffered hand. My purse is strapped across my body. Touching the small bag, I remember I have protection if I need it.

I glance at my uncle before following Lucas to the elevator. We ride in silence. Lucas is the only casual one among us. He's humming a tune and scrolling through his phone like he hasn't a care in the world.

When the elevator doors slide open on arrival, my uncle steps out ahead of us. Lucas gestures for me to go ahead of him, but we remain standing there for a moment as we study one another. I'm still awed by how similar he and Damian look but also how starkly different. The look in Lucas's darker eyes is one of those differences. It's harder. But also, more defensive or secretive as though he's protecting something. Like he's protecting himself.

I walk off the elevator and through the open front door of the apartment. It's familiar and foreign at once and I feel like a stranger. Like I don't belong here. Or maybe it's that I'm not quite welcome here. Was I ever truly welcome?

I turn to my uncle who looks so uncomfortable it's almost painful to watch him.

"Would you like something to drink?" Lucas asks me, crossing the room to the bar as though he owns the place.

"I'm fine. What's going on? Uncle Adam, why are you with him?"

Lucas pours himself and my uncle a whiskey. "Sit," he tells me.

It feels strange to be invited to sit in what was once my home, but when my uncle doesn't intervene, I take a seat, resting my hands on the purse in my lap.

My uncle remains anxiously standing against the far wall, not answering my question. Not even looking at me. I can't tell what he's thinking or where his head is. All I know is he looks about twenty years older than last time I saw him.

Once Lucas sets the bottle back on the bar, he turns to face me, expression curious.

"Isn't it early for that?" I gesture to their drinks.

Lucas shrugs a shoulder and sips. "Life is short. Carpe diem and all that shit."

"Why are we here? Why is my uncle here?"

"It's his house."

"Don't be a jerk. I called you because you promised to tell me the truth. Are you two working together against Damian or something?"

"We're doing what's best for you," my uncle says.

"All of you seem to think you're doing everything for my benefit, but I get the feeling none of you actually are."

Lucas glances at my uncle, then sits on the chair closest to mine, facing me. "Ask me your questions."

"You'll answer me truthfully?"

"I will answer the ones I'm able to truthfully."

"Why is my uncle here?"

"Because he's concerned for your safety," he says flippantly.

"Dick," my uncle mutters, then turns to me. "Damian did something that puts the foundation at risk. That puts you at risk."

I don't miss that he mentions the foundation before he mentions me.

"What did he do?"

"We'll get to that," Lucas answers after my uncle shifts his gaze to him almost in deference.

My uncle turns to refill his glass. I watch his

back, then shift my gaze back to Lucas. Okay. We'll get to it. I won't leave until I know.

"What happened to Annabel? The accident, I mean," I ask.

Lucas surveys me over his drink as though he's surprised that's what I ask. "She and Damian were playing in the solarium. She fell from the gangway and sadly lost the use of her legs after that fall."

I knew that from what Liam told me. It must have been awful for her. "I heard you say something yesterday. In Damian's study."

"I said many things. Which in particular are you curious about?"

"Something about accidents. A lot of them happening around Damian."

"I don't think he pushed her, if that's what you're getting at. He loved Annabel. But I know he felt guilty afterward. And I know our father blamed him for allowing it to happen. Blamed him for a lot of things." He sips his drink, looking over my shoulder. "That wasn't quite fair," he adds on, surprising me.

"Then why did you say that yesterday? About a lot of accidents happening around him?"

"Did you have your ear to the door?"

"You were loud."

"I was fucking with him. That's all, Cristina. And you should be asking different questions. Questions like what's going to happen to you after your year is up."

I feel the blood drain from my face.

"Christ," my uncle mutters. His face is a little flushed, the bulbous tip of his nose red like the last time. I wonder how much he's already drunk today.

Lucas stands to grab the bottle of whiskey and another tumbler. He pours a glass and hands it to me before resuming his seat.

"Don't worry, my brother won't go through with it."

I sip, shifting my gaze back to his once I've swallowed a good mouthful of the burning stuff. Courage. I need to be strong.

"With killing me?" I say, my voice higher than usual.

"Yes."

"That's what you intended? All these years?" It's surreal.

"Not me. My family. Well, my father to be more precise."

"Why? What would it do? I was a little girl when that accident happened. What would it do?"

He shrugs a shoulder so casually it pisses me off.

"It wouldn't bring her back, would it? It won't bring any of them back." I feel sick. It's a combination of being back in this house, Lucas and my uncle seemingly in cahoots, this conversation. Hell, it's this whole situation.

"We don't need to keep talking about it. You're obviously uncomfortable."

"How would anyone be comfortable with this topic? My God, are you even human, Lucas?"

"He won't do it. That's all. He has other plans."

That makes me stop. "What other plans?"

My uncle drinks.

Lucas just studies me.

"What other plans?" I push.

Nothing.

I exhale loudly and weave my fingers into my hair.

"I like it short by the way," he says.

I get to my feet, exasperated. When I turn to him, he leans back in his seat and puts his feet up on the coffee table as he sips his whiskey.

"You're pretty. My brother got lucky there, too."

"Are you for real? Is this a fucking joke to you? Is my life a joke?"

"I was just giving you a compliment. Relax."

"Relax? When you're spinning stories and confusing me even more than I already am?"

"I'm not spinning stories. That's my brother's area."

"This was a mistake." I walk to the door.

"Sit," he commands, his tone darker. Not joking.

I give him the finger and keep walking, unzipping my purse as I go and hurrying my step when I hear him get to his feet. I reach inside to take out the switchblade and push the button to open it just as he catches my arm.

"Get your hand off me!"

"Cristina!" My uncle's eyes grow wide.

Lucas looks down at the knife, cocking his head to the side. "Careful with that, sweetheart. It's sharp. I know. I made it." He sounds casual. Like me pulling a knife on him is nothing. "Now put that away before you hurt yourself and sit down."

"I said, let me go." He doesn't. I keep the blade pointed at him. "I agreed to get in that car with you because you promised to give me answers. Honest ones. You're jerking me around, and I don't like it. We're finished. This is a waste of time. You want to fuck with me just like your brother does. I don't know why I thought you'd actually tell me anything. And you." I turn to my uncle. "I don't know what you're doing with him. I'm not even sure I want to know!"

"I'm trying to save you," he says. "Put that away, Cristina."

"You're trying to save me? Or are you trying to save yourself? Tell me something, did you only take me in because they paid you to?"

"You're my brother's daughter. Of course not."

"But it didn't hurt that you got a better-than-new apartment and money and whatever else they gave you. And you made sure not to break any of their rules. Is that why I wasn't allowed to date? Or to even hang out with friends?"

"The point is moot, isn't it?" Lucas says.

I turn from my uncle to Lucas. "Fuck you. I'm done." I tug to get free, but he tightens his grip.

"Cristina," he says, voice so low it's more a rumble.

"Let. Go."

"Poor little rich girl. You finished feeling sorry for yourself?"

"I'm going to kill you."

"No, you're not."

Before I can even open my mouth to reply, he spins me around, locking my arms painfully behind my back. All it takes is a twist of his hand to have me crying out in pain as the knife falls to the Persian rug beneath my feet.

"Jesus Christ, you're going to break her arm! Let her go!"

My uncle's warning comes a beat too late as he's still across the room. Why isn't he hauling Lucas off me?

Lucas ignores him, leans his face so close to mine that I feel the scruff on his jaw against my cheek. "We're finished when I say we're finished. *You* summoned *me*. I came. Now, you do as you're told, and you sit your ass down." He releases me so abruptly that I stumble forward, almost falling.

"What the fuck is wrong with the Di Santo men thinking women should *do as they're told*? Do you know what year it is?"

"Cute."

Before I have a chance to scoop up the blade, he does. He closes it and tucks it into his pocket.

"You'll get that back when we leave. *If* you're good."

"That's mine!" I charge him.

He catches me easily, holding me at arm's length. "No, actually, it's Michela's. She only lent it to you."

"So I could protect myself against Damian, but maybe the one I need protecting from is you!"

He plants me on a chair and leans into me, hands tight around my wrists. "Do I need to tie you down?"

"Lucas," my uncle says in a tone that used to warn me when I was a child. It has no impact on Lucas, though.

"Because I might like that," he says, eyes falling to my lips as he licks his. "Maybe you will too."

"That's enough," my uncle says.

"Damian's going to kill you."

"Is that after you explain making plans to meet me. Getting into a car with me. I know how he punished Michela. What do you think he'll do to you?"

"He wouldn't do that!"

"No?"

"No."

He studies my face curiously, then exhales. "You know what? You're right. I actually don't think he would."

I stay in my seat, his comment unsettling, not comforting. Although I'm sure his intention isn't to make me feel comfortable.

"I was right," he says.

"Right about what?"

"That you have become a weakness to my dear, heartless brother. A chink in his armor." He resumes his seat. "Now let me clarify some things here, Cristina. First of all, I haven't lied to you. I've answered you truthfully. I am not your enemy. I have no reason to be."

"Did you know I was out in the woods that day?"

"Did I know you followed me? Yes."

"And you left me out there?"

"What would you have had me do? Drag you back to the house and lock you in your room? That's my brother's game."

"Except that this isn't a game. It's my life."

He doesn't comment.

"Did you set the fire?" I ask.

He snorts. "No, I did not."

"Did you help the people who did?"

"See, you're not asking the right questions."

"What do you mean?"

"That fire doesn't have anything to do with you. That has to do with Damian. He needs to learn not to cross certain people."

"Is he in danger?"

"Would you care?"

Would I?

"Are you ready for me to tell you why your uncle is here? Although, honestly, I'm starting to question his worth."

I swallow because I know this is going to be bad.

"I'll be honest, when I found out my brother's plan, well, it surprised even me, actually," Lucas continues. "It's cruel, really. But maybe his twisted brain makes it out to be merciful." He shakes his head.

I just stare at him, my heart racing, a sinking feeling in my stomach.

"Do you know why Damian married you, Cristina?"

I've wondered about this. About his answer when I've asked it. It seemed too altruistic for him to have done it to protect me without having something to gain from it himself.

"I know you received the bullshit about family rules and protecting you and blah, blah, blah and how noble would that make him if only it were true."

"What do you mean?"

"Is he protecting you now? From me?"

I glare at him.

"The Valentina Foundation, the Di Santo family has become heavily invested. He wouldn't want to let that go."

"I don't follow."

"What are the rules, Cristina? Who inherits the foundation and everything that comes with it?"

I glance up to find my uncle watching me with that same look he sometimes had when I was little. I never could figure out what it meant, but I hated it. It made me feel cold and unwelcome and mostly just bad. It feels the same now, but I think I'm starting to understand its meaning.

I think it's a sort of hate.

When I return my attention to Lucas, he's watching me curiously. I school my features as best I can. This man is dangerous.

Both of them are.

Hell, all of them are.

"It's just a charitable organization. There isn't much for personal gain," I say.

"It's a front. I think you can stop lying to yourself about that part already. But I'm not interested in that right now. Tell me who inherits."

"Firstborn."

"Right. And when your older brother died, who was next in line?"

"Me."

"And after you?"

"If I have kids, then my kids."

"And if you don't have kids?"

"Stop fucking around. Just tell her," my uncle says as I swallow the lump forming in my throat.

"To whom does the foundation go if you were to

meet an untimely end—or a timely one—and you did not have a successor?"

I look up to meet my uncle's hard eyes. "My uncle's line," I tell Lucas. "Him, then Liam."

"Unless you have an heir. Don't you think Damian would make a good daddy? Although he does share some of what I wouldn't consider Dad's best qualities."

My brain works hard to process, to make sense of what is senseless.

"No. You're wrong," I finally say, unable to come to terms with what I think he's saying. I look up at my uncle. "He's lying."

My uncle mutters a curse and runs a hand through his hair. It's Lucas who continues talking.

"Could be, I guess. Although my dear brother didn't deny it."

I shake my head and stand. "That's not right. And even if that's what he wanted I won't get pregnant. I'm on the pill, and he knows it. He just refilled my prescription even. That's not what he wants from me."

He cocks his head to the side. "Please tell me you're not that stupid."

Fuck.

I hug my arms to myself, suddenly chilled.

"What does he want then, Cristina?" Lucas asks me.

I look away. I don't know what Damian wants. All

I know is that he promised to let me go when he has it. His exact words.

"I have a doctor friend. I've already spoken to her. She'll give you a birth control shot that'll be good for three months."

"What?"

"Birth control shot. You've heard of those?"

"Of course. It's not..." I push my hands into my hair, then close my eyes to think. "I don't believe you. You're lying." I look up at him. "And I don't trust you."

"But you trust your uncle, right?"

I look at my uncle. "So that's why he's here? In order for you to have some backing? And you think because he's here I'll just take your word for it? News flash, Lucas. He betrayed me too, and he's blood."

Lucas sighs. "I'll be honest with you since no one else is. Yes, you're right. Your uncle is taking care of his interests—"

"She's my brother's daughter. I'm as invested in protecting her—"

"I don't think you are, Uncle," I cut him off.

He looks surprised to hear it. "I don't want to see you hurt, Cristina. No matter what."

"You don't have to take my word for any of this," Lucas says. "I did think having your uncle here would help make my case, but that was clearly a mistake. Although at least I know you're not as naïve as I assumed."

"You don't know anything about me, Lucas."

"Just think about it. Think about what makes sense." He finishes his drink, sets the empty glass down, and stands. "So, Damian refilled your prescription? That was nice of him. Damian is such a nice guy. Always doing things for other people and never thinking of his own personal gain."

Give me what I want, and I'll let you go.

I stand. "I want to leave."

"Suit yourself. Just remember what I said the next time my brother fucks you."

I flinch like he slapped me.

"You're lying."

"What reason would I have to lie? What would I gain by lying about this?"

"What do you have to gain by telling me?"

"What have I got to lose?" Lucas says with a shrug of his shoulders. "Let's go."

Give me what I want, and I'll let you go.

He never told me what he wants. I keep coming back to this.

"Wait," my uncle says.

I turn to him.

"Cristina, let him take you to the doctor. At least we can delay what Damian wants until we can figure out how to get you away from him."

"You didn't try to stop him before. Why would you now?"

"Because he has me," Lucas says. "Damian could

have crushed him before. But with my backing and the backing of the others that my brother is stupid enough to challenge, your uncle is in a much better position than he was. And yes, he is doing this out of self-interest. But in this case, his self-interest lines up with your safety."

I look at the both of them, but my mind is racing.

"Either way, even when blood betrays you, you must trust in greed. Your uncle doesn't want the foundation going to Damian. He'd lose all this." Lucas waves an arm around.

I bite the inside of my cheek, trying to gauge what's true and what's manipulation.

"Let me know where you want me to take you, the doctor or back to the café," Lucas says.

"Cristina," my uncle steps forward. "Let him take you to her office at least. You can see for yourself that she's a legitimate doctor. You may not have another chance."

I study him, try to see the man who raised me, but I can't. I turn to Lucas.

"I'll decide when I see her."

"Good enough. Let's go."

I follow him to the apartment door.

"Cristina," my uncle calls out.

I turn to him. "I'm trying to do what's best for you, for the family."

"No Uncle, you're doing what's best for you. Let's at least be honest about it."

I don't wait for him to answer but walk out the door and into the elevator to the garage, then to a different car than the one we came in. The windows on this one are tinted too. That's the only similarity.

"Why aren't we taking the car we came in?"

"Just a precaution in case we were followed."

We get into the car and pull out of the garage into busy Manhattan traffic.

He switches on the radio, humming along to a country song. Country. Didn't think he'd be into that. I look over at him and I think about how I don't know this man at all.

But how much do I know Damian?

I can only count on one thing. They are my enemies. They are all my enemies. Even my uncle.

But getting a birth control shot would buy me time just in case. If Lucas is lying, then it won't hurt anything. But if he's not and this is truly Damian's plan it could save me.

Dr. Laura Jones has a private practice on the seventh floor of a building midway between the apartment and the café. Lucas walks in with me, tells the receptionist his name and asks to see Dr. Jones. We bypass the women in the waiting room and are ushered straight into an empty office.

Dr. Jones walks in not five minutes later. She's in her mid-thirties, I guess, and seems to know Lucas.

"Lucas tells me you'd like a birth control shot,

and mentioned the circumstances are unique, which is why he's brought you to me."

I nod. "How long does it last?"

"Three months."

I bite my lip.

"If you're unsure," she says, glancing at Lucas. "We can do it another time." She checks her watch. "I have a full schedule. You can always make an appointment and return when you're ready."

"No." I won't have a chance to return and I can't get pregnant. I look at Lucas, try to gauge if he's being honest. What can he have to gain by lying to me about something like this? "I'll do it now," I tell the doctor.

"All right. Just take a seat and roll up your sleeve."

Lucas stands against the wall, watching as I do what the doctor says. Once the injection is prepared, she turns back to me.

I look at the needle. "That's big."

She smiles like you would to a child. "It won't hurt much. I'll numb the area."

A few minutes later, my arm is numbed, and she pushes the needle into it. It still hurts, but I bite back the pain. I feel the solution going in, and all the while, I wonder if I'm not making a mistake. Part of me hopes Lucas is the liar because I don't want it to be Damian.

"All done," the doctor says, and I glance at the

injection site, which has reddened. I roll down my sleeve and slip off the table, glad it's over.

"Thank you," I tell her as Lucas opens the door. I don't talk to him on the ride back.

When we get to the café, he double parks again. "It was fun. Let's do it again soon," he says.

"Let's not." I slip out of the car.

"Cristina," he calls out before I've closed the door.

When I turn back, he's got the switchblade in his hand.

"I promised to give this back if you were good. You may need it yet."

I take the knife, but before I can pull my hand away, he grabs it. His grip is firmer than I expect. His expression different than I've ever seen it. Hard but something else too. Something old. Something wounded. It's at odds with the man I'm coming to know.

"Take care with him, Cristina. He breaks everything he touches."

When he releases me, I back up a step. Feeling sick, like I want to throw up, I walk toward the café's entrance. If what he says is true, then is Damian trying to get me pregnant already? How cruel would that be? The cruelest. And I'd just told Liam that he isn't. That he doesn't hurt me.

What happens if he succeeds? What happens

after? Would he really keep his promise and let me go? Send me away?

And what? Steal my baby from me?

Lucas drives off when I open the café door.

I find Cash at a table. He's looking back at me. I shake my head, not entering. I let the door close. Hugging my arms around myself, I turn around and begin the long walk to the library, my one safe haven even if it is for just a little while. I have no doubt Damian's double-crossing soldier is following.

23

DAMIAN

When I'm back in the penthouse, I find Cristina in the master bathroom sitting in the tub, head back and eyes closed. I know why she doesn't open them when I find the bottle of vodka on the floor beside the arm hanging out of the bath.

Steam rises from the circular tub. I walk over, sit on the edge. Putting one finger in, I test the temperature.

She blinks her eyes open, appearing startled but then resigned as she reaches for the bottle, drinking straight from it.

I raise an eyebrow. "What's going on?"

"Nothing."

She glugs another generous swallow.

I take the bottle from her. I'd just opened recently and it's about half gone.

"That's mine," she says.

"You've had enough."

"No, I haven't. But I'm getting there." She closes her eyes and leans her head back again.

"Is this about last night?" I ask her, standing to take off my jacket. Rolling up my shirt sleeve, I reach in to pull out the plug.

"Hey. I'm taking a bath." She straightens, getting on her knees to search for the plug. She slips, splashing water onto the bathroom floor. I catch her before she smashes her face against the edge of the tub. She pulls away from me and attempts to plug the drain again.

"You're drunk. Come on. Out."

I grab a towel and unfold it. I notice the two months' worth of birth control containers lying open on the counter.

"What are you doing?" I ask her.

She looks at them then at me. "What are *you* doing?" she slurs.

All right. "Come on. Out, Cristina."

"No. Go away."

"Well, if you're not going to come out, then I'll come in."

"I don't want you."

"No, that's clear." I slip off my shoes and clothes. I guess she doesn't believe I'll do it until I'm in the tub, sliding behind her, holding onto her so she'll stay put.

"I don't want you here, Damian. I mean it."

"Why? This is nice."

"You're a jerk, that's why. Let me go."

"Listen—"

"I don't want to listen. Let go. You're hurting me."

I'm holding her upper arm. My grip isn't hard, but there's a bruise forming on the skin under my fingers. I lean closer, brushing my thumb over the slightly raised, reddened skin.

Shit. Did I do that?

"Listen," I say, moving my hand off the sensitive spot.

"I really don't want to hear any more of what you have to say."

"You haven't heard anything yet, Cristina."

She turns huge violet eyes to me. What I see inside isn't what I expect. Anger, I get. Being pissed at me, wanting to hurl things at me, I get. I was a dick last night. But what I see is hurt.

"Well, I don't want to hear at all."

"Look, I shouldn't have done what I did last night. Shouldn't have treated you like that. I'm sorry, okay?"

She sniffles, wiping the back of her hand across her face. "Not okay."

"Hey," I say, pulling her in to me.

I'm not sure if she yields to me, if it's that she's drunk, or just that the tub is slippery, but she lies back against my chest so I can wrap my arms around her. She's so light. So small. And a part of me is scared that my brother's right. That I'm going to break her.

"I was wrong. I'd had a bad day, I took it out on you, and I'm sorry. And just to be clear, I did not bring you here so I could have someone to fuck. That's not what you are to me, okay?"

She turns her head to rest her cheek against my chest like maybe she's too tired to hold it up. She brings her eyes to mine and I see the tears inside them.

"You never told me what you want," she says.

"What do you mean?"

"You said you'd let me go after I give you what you want. But you never told me what it is you want."

"That's gotten...complicated."

"What does that mean?"

I slide my hand down over her belly between her legs.

She makes a sound, then furrows her brows and tries to push my hand away.

"Shh. Look at me."

"Tell me. Just tell me."

"I meant one thing I said last night."

"What's that?"

"I like having you around."

Confusion creases her forehead.

I cup the back of her head, and when I rub her clit between my fingers, her mouth falls open.

"Damian—"

I pull her closer, kissing her open mouth. It's a very different kiss from last night. This is soft. This is gentle. This is me giving for a change. Because I know all I've done is take when it comes to her. And I know I'm not done taking.

I also know she doesn't deserve any of this.

The thing is, I can't let her go. Even now as I draw back and touch her cheek, I look at my hand against her pretty face, and I think about how ugly it is. How ugly I am. How monstrous my world.

And how I've plucked her from hers to force her into mine. To ruin her for my own selfish ends.

"Sometimes, I look at you," she says, licking her lips and swallowing as I bring her closer to orgasm. "I look at you and think about what you said the first night we met. The thing about monsters being out in the open so you can see their eyes."

I don't look away even though I should. Because I should shield my true nature from her.

Because what am I but a monster to do what I've done?

I told her it was for her own good when I forced that ring onto her finger. I think some part of me believed that, too, at the time.

At least I'd be saving her life.

No, not saving it. Let's be clear here. I'd be

sparing it. But if I go through with things, by the time I'm done, I'll have taken more from her than she can imagine. And she won't recover.

Something twists inside me at that. My brother is right. There's no denying it. I will break this girl because it's what I do.

I should let her go. But I won't. And it's not just that I don't want to.

I can't.

"Damian," she says, and when her eyes close, I watch a tear slide down her cheek. It twists something inside me, all her sadness. Her constant sadness.

"Cristina."

Her nails dig into my shoulders and she makes that sound. It's soft and quiet and just a whisper, a breath. All I can do is watch her. Watch her beautiful face as she's about to come.

But she abruptly opens her eyes then, pushing my hand off her, sending water all over the bathroom floor.

Turning to face me, she studies me for a long moment as she gets to her knees. I can't read her. For the first time since I've had her, I can't read her.

"Not like this," she says and stands. She looks down at me as water spills from her, feet straddling me, pussy at eye level. Wet and pink and making me harder than I already am.

She climbs out of the tub and walks to the door.

Glancing over her shoulder at me with an almost forlorn expression.

"What are you doing?" I ask.

"Not like this," she says, and I follow her out of the tub, grabbing a towel and walking into the bedroom.

I watch as she climbs onto the bed, getting on hands and knees, ass to me. She lowers herself onto her elbows and arches her back, knees wide enough to make my dick throb at the sight of her like this.

Like she's an offering.

An offering to me.

She lays her cheek on the bed and looks at me. "Fuck me, Damian. Fuck me like you want to fuck me. I know you're holding back. I feel it. I don't want you to anymore. I want you to show me who you are."

I drop the towel, my cock a steel rod. Placing my hands on her ass, I spread her wider, then lean my face down to kiss her, lick her from hole to hole.

"God, Cristina." I climb onto the bed behind her and situate myself between her open legs. She feels different than any other woman. She is different than any other woman.

"Do it," she demands, facing forward as if bracing herself. "Fuck me hard. Make it hurt, Damian. Make it hurt when you make me come."

Arousal overrules confusion as I slide into her wet cunt, moaning with the sensation of it, of the tight fit of her. I look at us like this, look at her take me, then touch my thumb to her asshole and hear her moan. I want that, too. I want to fuck that tight little hole too.

"Harder!"

"You want it hard?" I slap her ass, then dig my fingers into her hips and hold her steady, making her take my thrusts. "You like it like this?" I spank her again and again, watch her skin redden as I do, hear her suck in a breath, and feel her cunt drip around my dick.

Driving into her, I move one hand to her clit and push the thumb of my other hand into her asshole. She's tighter there and tenses momentarily. I curl my finger, hooking her.

"I'm going to fuck this tight little hole too. I'm going to watch your face when I take your ass."

She moans, arching her back for more.

"I'm going to come," she manages, pushing into me as I rub her clit, finger buried in her ass, my cock thrusting with punishing strokes into her pussy.

"Come. I want to feel you come with my dick in your pussy and my finger in your ass. Come."

"Make it hurt, Damian. Make it hurt."

Caught up in the fucking that's now become frantic, I do. I fuck her like she wants. Like I want. She cries out as she comes, her ass pulses around my finger, her cunt around my cock. When she looks back at me with those beautiful eyes, I lose it.

"God, I fucking love you," I groan.

I register the words. Does she? But any thought is overridden by this animal rutting, this beastly fucking.

When I come, I lose all thought, only feeling her from the inside. Only hearing her moans as I drill into her, pushing her flat onto her belly as my cock throbs deep inside her. Deeper than I've been yet, emptying inside her.

Spent, it takes minutes to roll onto my side. She turns her face to mine, our heads resting on the same pillow. The only sound in the room is that of our combined breathing, ragged and worn out.

We just look at each other for the longest time, her eyes soft, quietly watching. Does she see that monster, I wonder? Is that what she's searching for? She won't have to look hard.

It's when I touch her cheek to push back the hair that's matted to her face that everything changes. It's then she shutters her eyes and locks me out. The instant is so marked, I feel it like a chill.

It was too much too fast. "I hurt you," I say. Fuck. I should know better even if she asks for it. She doesn't know any better. I'm the first man she's been with.

"You will always hurt me," she says as if reading my mind. "You *should* always hurt me."

I get up on one elbow, a weight settling in my gut.

"Never make love to me or touch me like you did in the tub. Never be gentle."

I look at her, confused as fuck.

She sits up and looks down at me.

"I see you."

"What the fuck are you talking about?"

"I don't ever want to forget who you are. What you are. I don't ever want to forget that you're a liar and a monster. I want to see you with clear eyes, Damian Di Santo. And whatever feelings come up when you're fucking me, know that mine will never change. I will always hate you."

She spits the words and I'm dumbstruck as she wipes away a tear. Looking more hurt than angry, she slips off the bed and walks out of the bedroom, slamming the door behind her.

24

CRISTINA

I'd moved some things into another bedroom earlier. It's the one with the lock and although I already know he has a key, it makes me feel better to know it's one more barrier he'll have to get through to get to me. I don't even care that I'm walking naked down the hall. I'm sure at least one of Damian's soldiers is standing in the other room with a clear view of me.

It's then that I realize something.

Lucas never answered one of my questions. It's been niggling at me all afternoon but with all the other crap going on, I'm only now getting to it.

When I'd asked Lucas if he'd set the fire, he said he hadn't, and I believe him. I think he's too smart to actually do it himself.

But I know what I saw, and I can't doubt myself.

Not now. Not when everyone around me is using me to get what they want.

Now that I know about the fire, I wonder if what he was carrying out there was gasoline. When I asked him if he'd helped the men who'd set the fire, he deflected me expertly. He asked me a question in return, distracting me. And I'd so easily been distracted.

In a way, what I learned today has made me accept my situation. My captivity. And strangely, I've made some peace with it. Maybe it's knowing the truth, as horrible as that truth is. Maybe it's just finally having all the pieces and seeing them as they are, not as I want them to be.

Not as I want *him* to be.

Because I do want them to be different. And I want him to be different.

I didn't miss what Damian said to me in there. I think it hurts more because he did say it. Because I do want to hate him, and if I say it enough times, maybe I will. If he hurts me enough, maybe I will.

Maybe one day, I'll grow a brain and hate him like I should.

I looked at some of the birth control pills and compared them to my original pills. Although I couldn't see any difference, I'm not sure what Lucas said isn't true. It makes sense.

My arm throbs at the injection site. I look at it. The skin is an angry, swollen, red, and the bruise has darkened. I touch it lightly, but it's so tender I pull my hand away.

I'm just picking up the key I'd put into the nightstand drawer to lock the door when it opens. Before turning around, I wrap my hand around the hilt of the blade instead.

I'm not surprised but my breath still hitches when I turn around to face a very angry Damian.

"What the fuck was that?" he asks, eyes falling to the switchblade I haven't opened.

Keeping it in my hand, I pick up my robe to slip it on. I don't bother to tie it closed. All the while, I'm very aware of the cum growing sticky on my thighs.

He's put on a pair of jeans but is naked otherwise. When I see him like this, I can see him working in that shed. See his body slick with sweat as he painstakingly carves the intricate details on the Gates of Hell doors.

"If you open that, we have a problem. A bigger one than you made inside."

I meet his eyes, stormy, a tumultuous gray. When he approaches me, I don't have any room to back up.

He takes my wrist lightly. "Are we going to have a problem?" He squeezes just a little, showing me that if I fight him, I'll lose.

"No," I say, turning my hand over for him to take the switchblade from me.

"Good." He pockets it. I guess he's not risking it. "What the fuck was that, Cristina?"

"Which part?" I ask, sounding strangely calm even though my heart is racing.

"The part where you ask me to fuck you hard, come, then call me a monster and walk out."

"Aren't you a monster? Isn't that what you've been trying to tell me? Isn't that what you warned me about when I was just ten years old?" I feel my eyes warm with tears, and I know he sees them, too. I wish I was harder, more resilient.

I wish I were a monster too.

"Don't you see anything I do? Hear anything I say?" he asks.

He told me he loved me. I heard that. But it was in the throes of fucking, so I call that the unreliable ramblings of a man thinking with his dick.

Yet something inside me twists because I am just stupid enough to want it to be real. I am just pathetic enough.

"I think that apart from Scott and Liam, every single man I have ever known wants something from me." I walk away, needing space. When my back is turned, I wipe my face.

He doesn't let me get far though. He's standing in front of me again in the next second.

"Does this have to do with your impromptu meeting with my brother today?"

He must see the shock on my face.

"You didn't think Cash was the only soldier I sent with you, did you?"

"You said—"

"I told you I'm not going to let anything happen to you. That means anyone who'd hurt you. Even my own blood."

"You were having me followed even though you sent me with a soldier?" I ask, remembering Liam's comment about the goons out on the street, and how I'd dismissed it when he'd suggested they were Damian's men.

"Four additional soldiers were tailing you. That's how I knew about Liam yesterday."

"Did you do this for my own good, like everything else you apparently do?"

"One man—and a disloyal one at that—wouldn't be able to stand against an attack. I wasn't going to take any chances with you. They'll hurt you to get to me. Don't think they won't try."

It takes me a minute to digest those last words.

"And if you're wondering, Cash has been dealt with," he says.

"What do you mean 'dealt with'?"

"I don't tolerate traitors, Cristina. I hope you won't become one."

The way he says the word traitors and the way he's looking at me make me shiver.

"If you think me a traitor, will you deal with me like you do your men?" My belly quivers, my courage fading.

He narrows his eyes to search my face. He's not

angry, though. He's curious. And something else. Something I can't quite put my finger on. Hurt, maybe?

Don't be stupid.

"You're my wife. I'll deal with you differently *if* I have to. But I hope I won't have to."

It's strange when he talks about me being his wife. It doesn't fit. I'm his wife because he needs me to be. Period. If Lucas is telling me the truth. If my uncle is. Even if Lucas would lie out of hatred for Damian, why would my uncle?

"Now do you want to tell me about the poison Lucas spewed into your ear? Because I'm guessing that's the cause for your little show in there."

He lays his big hand on the flat of my belly and nudges me backward. When I reach the wall, he leans in close. He eyes the expanse of exposed skin and my mouth goes dry. I'm hyper aware of him being so close. Hyper aware of his body. His strength. His heat.

"And as far as that goes," he starts, licking his lips and returning his eyes to mine. "I did like it. I liked you waving your little ass at me. I'm happy to bend you over and fuck you raw anytime you like. And like I said in there, I will fuck your asshole too. Just make sure I don't do it as punishment, or you will know pain."

I swallow so hard it's audible.

He exhales a short, sharp breath, then steps

back, looks around the room, and pulls a chair forward that had been placed against the wall.

"Sit."

"Why?"

"Because I said so." This time, he doesn't wait for me to move. He puts me into the chair roughly. When he releases me, I stay there.

He's bigger and stronger than I am. There's no way I will beat him physically and I won't waste my energy trying.

"Now tell me what you did with my brother."

"Didn't the men you had following me already tell you?"

"Unfortunately, they couldn't see into your uncle's apartment."

"How can two brothers hate each other so much?"

"Betrayal is betrayal, blood or not. Talk. And just to be clear, you get one chance to tell me the truth. If I even think I smell a lie, you will lose the few privileges you have gained."

"Like being allowed out of my room, you mean? Only to be followed and spied on by your goons?"

He braces his hands on the arms of the chair and leans his face toward mine. "Talk."

"I wanted to see my uncle, so Lucas brought me to him. I didn't think you'd allow me to go, after all."

"No, you're right. And there's a reason for it. It

was nice of my brother to play taxi driver for you. He's a nice guy, though. It's what he's known for."

"Funny, he said the same thing about you."

"Did you call him to meet you? Remember, I can check your phone, but I'd rather we learn to trust each other."

"Trust each other? Are you serious?"

"Did you call him to meet you?"

"Yes."

"How did you get his number?"

"He gave it to me yesterday. When he barged out of your study after your argument. He told me when I was ready to hear some truth, I should call him. Given how things went with you and me the night before, I figured I'd take him up on his offer."

He grits his teeth and some stupid part of my brain tries to remind me how he apologized for that.

"Don't keep me in suspense. What did you want to see your uncle about?"

"Liam said he'd been drinking, and I wanted to see for myself how bad it's become. I thought if I talked to him—"

"Bullshit. You just lost your phone."

"No!"

He sits on the edge of the bed and folds his arms across his chest. "Start again."

"I want that phone. It's my only way to talk to Liam."

"And I told you not to lie to me. Start. Again. And remember there's more I can take away."

"Why do you even care? My uncle is just a pawn."

"Whose pawn?"

"Yours. Lucas's."

"Well, you at least got that right. Your uncle is unimportant. Just a pawn, like you said. Which tells me you didn't call my brother to see your uncle."

He reads me like a book. "No, not specifically. But he was there in the car when Lucas came to meet me. I thought we'd just talk at the café, but Lucas said he brought my uncle so I'd leave with him." That's half of the truth. I will omit the other half.

"What did my brother have to tell you?"

"You don't answer any of my questions, Damian. I needed answers."

"And you thought you could trust him to give them to you?"

"I don't think I can trust either of you. Hell, I can't trust any of you, not even my uncle. Every one of you will use me to get what you want."

He doesn't deny it but remains silent, waiting for me to continue.

"Do you know what I wanted to ask you about the other night?"

"What?"

"I wanted to ask you why you own my house."

A blink out of rhythm is all that gives away his surprise. He is the master of schooling his features.

"Liam has a gift for finding out all kinds of things people don't want you to know about them," I say. "That's what I wanted to ask you about before you humiliated me."

"I apologized for that. I can't go back in time and erase what happened."

"No, you can't. Why did you buy it?"

His forehead wrinkles and he takes a deep breath in then out before answering. "I don't know, Cristina."

"How can you not know?"

"Believe it or not, I wasn't fully on board with what my father did to yours or the way he did it, but I don't have an answer to your question. When I do, I promise to tell you."

I don't know why I believe him, I do though, and it loosens something inside me. Softens it.

But I can't let that happen. I can't soften.

I look away from him. I need space. I need to think. To steel myself.

"Did you tell Lucas about the house?" he asks.

"No."

"Good. Don't. What did he tell you that turned you against me overnight?"

"Do you really think he did that all by himself?"

"I'm trying to do right by you."

"Are you?"

"Yes, I am. Now what did my brother tell you?"

"He told me about Annabel. About the accident."

"I'm sure he painted a pretty picture."

"He actually said it wasn't your fault. He said your dad blamed you, but that you loved Annabel and you'd never hurt her."

This seems to confuse him. It absolutely silences him for a long minute at least.

"Did you think I had hurt Annabel?" he asks appearing genuinely surprised.

I consider this, then look back at him. "No. Never."

"Well, that's something we can work with."

"He said what you want is the foundation, Damian. At any cost."

He studies me and when he doesn't even try to deny what I'm saying, that twisting is back. It's more like a fist in my chest now.

"Does your silence mean it's true?" I ask.

"It's complicated."

"Like us?"

"Yeah, like us."

I try for a chuckle, but it comes out choked. I need to get out of here and be alone for just a minute. Just long enough to lock these feelings away. Long enough that he won't see what this is doing to me or how weak I am.

I get up, turning toward the bathroom.

"Sit back down. We're not done."

"I'm done. We're done." I feel the first sting of tears as I take a step away.

"I said sit back down."

I don't. I keep moving. And the instant he's on his feet, I break into a run. It's instinct. Fight or flight. I always choose flight.

"I said sit back down," he says, grabbing my arm.

The instant he does, a sharp pain cuts through me, and I cry out.

We both stop, look at where he's got hold of me, where I'm trying to pry him off.

"It hurts."

He loosens his grip but steps closer, pushes the robe off my shoulder and brushes two fingers over the slightly raised skin. He peers closer.

"What is this?" he asks. "The skin's hot."

I look at it too, see the little hole the needle left, then try to pull my robe up before he sees it. "It must be a spider bite or something."

When he presses on it, I suck in a hissing breath.

"We need to get it looked at. It might be infected."

"It's fine," I say, trying to tug my arm free. "It's nothing. It won't hurt if you don't grab me like you did."

Commotion in the hallway has us both turning to the door, and a second later, there's a knock.

"Damian," it's Tobias.

Damian releases me. I close my robe as he checks his watch, then opens the door.

Tobias glances at me, then at Damian. "We have a location."

"Give me two minutes."

Tobias nods, and he's gone, closing the door behind him.

Damian turns back to me. "We'll continue this when I'm back."

"No. I'm done. *We're* done. There's nothing to continue."

"If you want to sleep in here tonight, that's fine." He continues as if I haven't spoken at all. "But when I get back, you and I will talk. Come tomorrow, you're in my bed every night. Period." He walks to the door, hand on the doorknob.

"You demand everything of me and give me nothing."

He pauses, and I hear him exhale, but then he opens the door.

"At least tell me one thing, Damian. Just one."

He turns around and raises an eyebrow, hand still on the doorknob

"What do you want?" I ask.

"Be more specific."

"You never told me that. What is it that I need to give you for you to let me go? Because if your brother is telling the truth, if it's truly the foundation, then there's only one way you can get it and let me go at the same time. And I don't want to believe you're monster enough to do that."

He stares back at me and his entire body tenses before my eyes. It's a bigger reaction than I expect.

That fist in my chest tightens its grip on my heart, squeezing the life out of it.

This betrayal hurts. Hurts like nothing else.

Damian closes the door.

"My brother is a liar, Cristina," he says more calmly than I expect, given his physical reaction. "He's manipulating you to get to me. He will do anything to destroy me."

"Why?"

"It's complicated."

"That's your answer for every question you don't want to answer."

"Look—"

"Just explain it to me. I can follow. Please."

He considers, steps toward me, then stops. I know he's made his decision when I hear his sigh.

"Because he was supposed to have what I have. He was the firstborn son technically, or at least my father chose him because he was bigger than me at birth. It'd be something for him to do. I don't know. I'm not even sure I was the backup plan. An unwelcome surprise maybe when they realized my mom was pregnant with twins. I think my father hated us both, truth be told. I think my father is only capable of hate. He thought us weak from day one. Holding each other's hands rather than having them around each other's throats.

"Anyhow, he chose Lucas, but Lucas—he wasn't always like this. When we were growing up, he was the gentle one."

I find that hard to believe; not that I'd ever accuse Damian of being gentle.

"And to teach Lucas to be the man he needed him to be, a man like my father is, he made it his habit to hurt me while Lucas watched. It's more effective that way. Did you know that? To hurt the thing the one you really want to hurt loves."

Loves.

They'll hurt you to get to me.

"Until Lucas finally started doing it himself, that is. Until he learned. Do you know *I* had to comfort *him* afterward?" He shakes his head.

"At least when it was my brother doing the beating, I guess you could say he took it easier on me or tried to, and I know he felt terrible. I know it chipped away at him. I think he started to hate himself before I realized what was happening to him."

He takes a break, pushes his hand into his hair, and in his eyes, I see he's miles away. Back in the past maybe. After a long moment, his eyes refocus on mine.

"For every misstep any of my siblings made, guess who took the punishment? And thing is, Lucas was the creative one. He was the one who got me into the woodworking. He was the softer of us. Always. He wasn't ever cut out to be the man my father wanted and expected him to be. Never had it in him. Hell, I far surpass him in that area. I'd have made my father proud and I hate myself for that.

"But something was happening all those years that I didn't see. Lucas's resentment of me grew at the same pace as his self-hatred. The accident, the fact that I was driving, what happened to him, Lucas blames me. Thinks it was my revenge for what he did to me even though that's his own guilt. I never blamed him, not really. I knew who he really was underneath it all.

"I'm not even sure he wants any of this, but he cannot let me have it." He takes a breath, then runs a hand through his hair. "And you know what? I still don't hate him. I wish I did. I try to. I miss him. I miss my brother the way we were before our father made us what we've become. But I know it's too late to get that back because something died inside him the night of the accident. No, that's not right. It was already dead by then. That accident, what it did to him, it's what turned him rotten."

I reach out to touch him, but he puts up his hand to stop me.

"Annabel's death was what pushed us all to the place we've come to. And I don't think there's any going back. Not for any of us."

His gaze shifts to the scar on my face.

Everything always comes back to that. To that damned accident.

He reaches out a hand and tucks a strand of hair behind my ear. He brushes his knuckles over the scar on my lip and a storm that's been brewing for a decade darkens his eyes.

"The end is coming, Cristina."

I shudder.

"And I won't be able to stop it. I won't be able to stop the storm my brother is bringing."

He drops his hand, pupils focusing on me again.

"Can't you walk away? Just leave it all?"

"That's the thing. Whatever it is, I need to see it through. Finish it and put the past to rest. Bury it finally."

I shudder.

It's silent for a long moment before he speaks again.

"You still want me to tell you what I want? I will."

I search his eyes, my heart racing, trying to process everything he just told me. Trying to reconcile this man who feels pain, who feels remorse and sadness, with the monster Lucas accuses him of being, the monster he doesn't deny being.

I nod because I believe he'll tell me now.

"I lied when I said I would let you go. No, that's not right. I don't think it was a lie then. But it's become one."

"What do you mean?"
"You don't see?"
I wait, my mouth dry.
"I can't let you go, Cristina."
"Why?"
"Because I love you."

25

DAMIAN

I drive over an hour to fucking Conshohocken, Pennsylvania, to find my brother drinking himself into a stupor in the seedy room of a strip club. One woman kneels between his legs sucking his dick, while two others tongue each other for his viewing pleasure.

I don't want to think about what I'm touching as I step into the private room.

"They don't have strip clubs in the city?" I ask.

"Brother," he says, lifting his bottle of tequila in greeting. "Thought you might drop by."

The room is the size of my walk-in closet. Mirrors make up each wall and the lighting is Red Light District red. A whore's red.

"Grab one," he says, gesturing to the girls who have their tongues in each other's mouths. "I'd offer you this one, but her cock sucking skills are superior.

He glances down to the naked girl who's currently swallowing his dick. He winks at her and she closes her eyes to get back to work.

Women like this, I never get the draw. I don't think I could even get it up if this is all that's on offer. I wouldn't want to.

"Out," I tell the girls.

Tobias signals for two soldiers who enter and take the girls sucking face by the arms and haul them to their feet.

"Hey!" one says, stumbling over someone's foot.

"Hold on. They did good work," Lucas calls out as he swallows more tequila. "Here, girls." He hands them each some money from the pile of hundreds on the small table beside him before they're removed.

"Get her out, too," I tell Lucas.

He looks down at her. "Come on, sweetheart. You can finish me off after my brother's given me a talking-to."

She places her hands on his thighs, gives him one final suck, then slowly stands, waving her ass at me as she bends forward to kiss my brother deeply.

He reaches for several hundred-dollar bills and hands them to her. "Don't go far. I'm going to need to fuck something when he's done. I'd like for it to be your face," he says with a slap to her ass.

"You always had a way with the ladies," I tell him as the girl leaves.

"She's no lady."

"Got that right."

"I think she'd fuck me if I didn't have a face left at all. I like girls like that. Easier than the ones who run away screaming." Any joking vanishes from his expression.

Tobias leaves. I know he'll stand just outside while I talk to Lucas.

"Drink?" he asks, gesturing to the bottle as he puts his dick away.

Taking it, I drink a swallow. Quality is okay, not great. Probably the best this place stocks. But I know when he's drinking tequila, it's bad. He used to do it when we were younger too. Tequila hits him harder. I guess he needs the oblivion.

I think about what I told Cristina. About everything I told her. I've never spoken a word of that to a soul. Not once. No one knows about how we grew up.

Taking a seat, I rest my head against the back of the tall bench.

"How did we get here?" I ask.

"We were always going to get here," he says, sounding remarkably sober. Maybe there isn't enough tequila in the world to send him into oblivion at this point. "Heard what you did to the Clementi brothers."

I went old school but kept my word to their

father. They're alive. Each only had one kneecap blown out. And they got to choose which one.

"You here to do the same to me?" Lucas asks, turning to me. "Or worse?"

I'm surprised. I guess I expected him to deny his involvement. And when I look at him, in his eyes I see what I used to see when we were younger. Especially at the beginning when he finally took over beating me while our father watched with pride in his eyes.

Pain. And fear. But more pain.

I reach for the papers that I've folded into three and tucked into my jacket pocket. I set them on the table beside the money.

"You supplied the drugs."

"That's not accurate."

"You put up the money to do it."

He swallows three gulps of tequila. Again, no denial. I get the feeling he's tired.

"Does Father know?"

"Does it matter?"

"Matters to me."

"No."

"What did you tell the Clementi brothers to get them to agree?"

"Told them the truth. You're not interested in moving drugs, but I am, and there's money in drugs. Considering my position, I needed a trustworthy player."

"You mean a gullible one."

"Most people are gullible." He pauses, never taking his eyes off me. "They hate you, Damian. They think you take more than your fair share."

"I take the risk. The ships are mine. What was your intention? What did you expect or want to happen?"

"The feds would have received an anonymous tip."

Well, at least he doesn't lie.

"You realize that would ground the fleet at the very least and for quite a while. Feds are already chomping at the bit to put us out of business."

"Us?"

"The family. Like it or not, you are a part of this family."

"But you're the boss."

"And that burns you up."

"Interesting choice of words."

"How much did you pay Cash to get my wife into your car."

"Your wife walked into my car of her own free will. And before you ask, *she* called *me*. Not the other way around."

"How much?"

"Not enough for what you did to him, I'm guessing."

"Is there anyone else? Any other traitors I should know about?"

"You cleaning house?"

I don't answer.

"I'll let you figure that out for yourself," he says. "Let it be a surprise."

"It doesn't have to be this way between us, Lucas."

"What other way can it be, Damian?"

I take the bottle from him and drink.

"What happens now? We going out back? The alley here is pretty suitable for the kind of work we do."

I put the bottle down.

Shit.

"I deserve it, don't I?" he asks, not quite looking at me anymore. "I beat the shit out of you. Repeatedly. When you were powerless. I can fight, at least. Tables are finally turned. Bet you've been waiting for that."

"I haven't been."

"And you know what else? I'd have done what you did to Michela too if he'd told me to. Probably worse than you did, if I'm honest. I know what I'm capable of."

"What he made you capable of."

We sit in silence for a long minute, the only sound the beat of music beyond the door.

"Can I ask you something?" he asks, surprising me.

"Yeah."

"Do you love her?"

I'm caught off guard. I don't expect that.

He studies me while I absorb his question. I try to figure out when it happened, when I fell in love with her. When she went from being the object of my vengeance to becoming something—someone—I took care of.

Someone I care for.

Hell, maybe it was a decade in the making.

I meant what I said to her. I won't let anyone hurt her. I will protect her. And it's not for what she can give me. Because I have what I want. Her.

"Not going to answer?" He takes a swig of tequila. "I have a request."

"What's that?"

"You be the one to do it. You pull the trigger."

Fuck.

Christ.

Fuck.

"I thought you'd found some peace when you stayed away so long after Annabel," I say.

He shakes his head. "Not even close." His shoulders are slumped, and I'm not sure if it's tequila or life that has him looking like he does. "You?" he asks, surprising me when he turns to look at me.

I smile. "Peace? In the Di Santo house? Not even close."

He smiles a sad smile. "I'm ready. I want this. I want it over. I've wanted it over for a long time."

I look at my twin brother. The brother I don't recognize anymore and not just because of the scars. Hell, maybe I haven't recognized him in a long time. Since we were kids.

I stand. "I'm not going to hurt you."

He looks up at me, eyebrows furrowing together.

"Disappear, Lucas. Don't let me see you again. Just disappear and find some peace." I walk to the door, push the curtain aside, then begin to step through.

Tobias stands aside. I know he'll disapprove. He knows Lucas and doesn't have any of the attachments I do. In a way, I wish Lucas were to me what Tobias is. A friend. A man I trust.

"Hey!" Lucas calls out.

I keep moving.

"Wait," Lucas says.

I turn back to find him on his feet.

"Find some peace?" he asks, disbelief on his face. "You think there's peace for me? You think I want to go back out there and find fucking peace?"

"I don't know what you want from me." I take a step out.

"You owe me this," he yells at my back.

I turn to study him. My brother. He doesn't hide his hate for me, and I realize at that moment that he's far past finding peace.

And I understand something about him that scares me more than anything else ever could.

"You fucking owe me," he repeats a little more calmly.

He wants to die. My brother wants to die.

And he wants me to be the one to do it.

"I don't owe you that."

26

CRISTINA

Because I love you.

The words won't stop repeating.

After I take a shower, I'm lying on the bed in the dark, wanting to sleep but wide-awake. It's the middle of the night and my brain is whirling. After what he told me, how he told me, and what I saw in his eyes, I'm baffled.

Damian is a monster. He warned me long ago and I never doubted it. Not even in the moments I took shelter in his arms. But he's more than that.

The thing about the beatings, I can't begin to wrap my mind around that. His family is fucked up, their relationships enmeshed and unhealthy. But that? A father having one son beat the other? A father turning brother against brother and in that way? I just can't understand. I can't process.

But it's what he said last that I keep coming

back to.

Because I love you.

He loves me. And I feel a strange joy knowing it.

Without thinking, I reach to scratch my arm. It's itchy and painful, and I think Damian may be right that it's infected. But it's not a spider bite.

Because I love you.

My phone buzzes under my pillow. He left in such a hurry he must not have remembered to take it from me. I'm sure he will tomorrow, but for now, I sit up, squinting my eyes as they adjust so I can read the text.

Liam: Put on the news.

Me: What?

Liam: Just turn on the TV.

I look around for the remote and see it on the nightstand on the opposite side of the bed. Reaching over, I grab it and push the power button.

CNN comes on and I watch as a news anchor speaks while the headline ticker scrolls across the bottom of the screen. Red lights flash and the aerial image shifts as the helicopter with the camera circles the fire fighters battling the fire on a loaded container ship.

The TV is muted so I switch on the lamp beside the bed in order to find the volume button and turn it up.

The scene has changed to a different location where a fire rages on board another ship.

I drop the remote and call Liam who picks up on the first ring.

"What's going on?"

"Those are Damian's ships. Three different ports."

Something on the TV explodes and I gasp.

"Philadelphia, New York, and Miami were hit. I'm guessing Genoa's hit too. Possibly Rotterdam."

I hear him typing madly.

"I don't understand. His ships?"

"His whole fleet is under attack."

Just then, the door smashes open, and a soldier I don't recognize enters.

I let out a little scream, dropping my phone as he rushes into the room, machine gun slung over his shoulder. He holds out his phone to me.

"Cristina."

I hear Damian's voice.

"What's going on?" I ask, taking the phone.

"We're under attack. You need to leave the penthouse now. No time to pack anything. Just go. Now."

"What? Where? And where are you?"

"I'll call you as soon as I can." I hear sirens in the background as he disconnects the call.

"We need to go," the soldier says and stands at the door.

"I need to get dressed."

"No time."

He pushes the covers off. I'm wearing a tank top

that comes to the tops of my thighs. That's all.

I grab the robe as he looks down and sees that I'm barefoot.

"There," I say, pointing at my boots. He hands them to me, and I slip my sockless feet inside. I've barely tied the robe when he takes my arm and rushes me through the hall, into another room where more soldiers wait.

We climb into what appears to be a service elevator and I ride down with three heavily armed men.

"I forgot my phone!" I say, realizing it only after the elevator starts moving.

"We can't go back," he says.

He takes hold of my arm again and, when the elevator doors open, we're not in the elegant front lobby but at the back of the building. We rush through what must be storage units. I shudder when we step outside because the thin robe and nightie offer no protection against the cold.

The soldier hurries me out onto a receiving area where a dark SUV waits, engine running. Another soldier steps forward as we near the end of the raised platform. I'm handed off from one to the other as if I'm a thing and lifted off my feet to be placed into the back of the SUV. We leave the soldier who brought me down and another one climbs in beside me. The driver takes off before he's even closed the door.

"I need your phone. I need to call Damian."

"Damian's busy. He'll call you when he can."

"Where are we going?" I ask frantically.

"Safehouse."

"Where?"

He doesn't answer, but when I shiver, he takes off his jacket and puts it over my shoulders.

"Thank you."

He nods.

I watch out the window as we drive out of the city and head north. I think for a minute he's taking me back to the main house Upstate, but then we take a turn, and I realize where we're going.

I'm surprised.

Shocked, actually.

My guess is confirmed not twenty minutes later as we drive through the gates of the house I lived in for the first ten years of my life.

It takes me a moment to process the emotions that come up as I look around the gardens and the large brick mansion, while the driver navigates the circular drive. It's well maintained. The shrubs in the garden, which my mother kept in an English style, are bigger, but almost the same as when I was little. I can just see our swing set and the treehouse our father had built for Scott and me. The last time I climbed into it was just after the accident.

This neighborhood on Staten Island is absolutely still compared to Damian's penthouse in the city.

When the SUV comes to a stop, the three men file out.

Someone opens the front door. Another soldier.

This is Damian's safe house? Is that why he didn't want me to tell Lucas?

One of the men opens my door and I slip out. It's so quiet here. You never realize how much you miss the quiet until you hear it again. Feel it again. It's the strangest thing.

The man gestures for me to go to the front entrance.

I look at it for a moment.

The house was never as still when I was growing up as it is now. Scott and I were always running around and creating a commotion.

My heartbeat isn't frantic, but it has picked up. I haven't been here in over eight years. Not since after the funeral luncheon my uncle organized for my father. That day, I was like a ghost in my own home.

Liam had come. He was around eight years old then. I wouldn't go near the study. It was off-limits anyway. My uncle had locked the door, but even being near it, down the hall from it, it upset me.

I knew my father hadn't killed himself. I knew those men had killed him. And I hadn't told a soul. I couldn't.

Liam and I had sat in my room for most of that

afternoon. He'd even helped me pack some toys to bring with me to his house. My new home.

"Mrs. Di Santo?"

I blink, looking at the man in confusion when he repeats it.

Mrs. Di Santo. That's me.

"We need to get you inside."

I nod and follow him toward the front door. Taking the three steps, I look up at the tall lampposts outside. They'd still been on that night. They must have only cut the power inside the house.

A gust of wind chills me as I get to the front door. I hug my borrowed jacket closer. Emotion and memory collide the instant I step into the foyer. It's like walking into a ghost room. Although it's clean, most of the furniture is covered with dust cloths. Those pieces that aren't, that the soldiers are obviously using, like the sofa in the living room and the dining room table and chairs, I recognize. It's all the same. He hasn't changed anything. Even the smell of the place is the same.

The door closes behind me and I jump.

Looking back, I see the man who gave me his jacket, so I slip it off and hand it back to him. "Thanks again."

"No problem."

"How long will we be here?"

"Until we get the all clear. Kitchen is stocked if you need anything. You're free to go to your old room. Please let me know where you will be at all times."

"What's your name?"

"Joseph."

"Joseph. Okay. How many men are here?"

"Just three. But you're safe. No one knows this location and the gates are locked."

"Do you know what's going on?"

"There were explosions on four of the shipping yards that house Di Santo ships."

"Was anyone hurt?"

"I don't know."

"Is Damian hurt?"

"No, ma'am."

"Can I use a phone?"

"No, ma'am." His phone rings then and he excuses himself.

I bite my lip. I want to call Liam. He must be worried. I just dropped the phone.

Looking down the hall toward the study door makes my heart beat faster. My breathing tightens as I remember Damian that night. I can almost picture us standing here in the hallway. I can almost feel what I felt then.

There used to be a phone in my dad's study. I wonder if it's still there. I can use that to call Liam.

I walk down the hall toward it, trying to keep the emotions that are flooding me from taking me under. I have to do this. See this.

Family photos hang along the walls here and all over the house. It was my mom's project. She'd add to the collections every Christmas, having us pick our favorites and helping her frame them. She took great photos. It was a hobby of hers.

I stop to look at each one we pass.

We're at the beach in this one. I must be six or seven, and everyone looks so happy. Scott, my dad, and I are soaked from a swim. I have on goggles too big for my face and a snorkel. Scott is biting into a huge wedge of watermelon, his goggles on top of his head, feet still in the flippers. His hair's almost as long as mine. He hated going to the barber.

It's been years since I've seen these. Since I've thought about any of this. Since I've wanted to remember. All these years, it was easier to block it all out. Just not think about it because it was so painful. And it's still painful although I'm more numb now. But underneath that layer of numbness, hurt and loss still throb.

I guess I've never really grieved for them. I don't think I knew how. And after the accident, my father wasn't capable of helping me through it when he was dealing with so much grief himself.

But I'm not sure you ever get over the death of your family, do you? Is Damian over the loss of his sister or mother?

"Ma'am."

I jump, finding Joseph standing behind me. He's

different than Cash was. He walks and talks like a trained soldier. For some reason, I know he's loyal to Damian and it makes me feel safer.

"Why don't you go upstairs and get some rest. We'll wake you if anything changes."

"Can I make a call?"

"No, ma'am."

"I just want to let my cousin—"

"It would compromise our location."

"Can you just ask Damian at least?"

"Shall I escort you up, ma'am?"

I press my lips together and exhale. "No, that's fine. I know the way."

Without another word, I turn and head up the stairs.

The curtains in my room are closed. I flip the light switch and the lamp beside my bed goes on, bathing the room in warm yellow light.

I stand with my back against the door, my hands behind me, as I take it in.

Scott's bed is in one corner and mine stands against the other. We were so close we'd wanted to share a room. His bed is covered in a dust cloth but mine is made in bedding I recognize.

I go to it, pull back the blanket and lean my head down to smell the sheet. It smells clean and fresh, ready for me to crawl into. Has he had it maintained all these years? Why?

Before I walked in here, I'd peeked into my

parents' bedroom to see if I could use the phone there. But the furniture was covered over with dust cloths similar to the one that covers Scott's bed. And the phone was gone.

I turn to the wall of dolls and remember the one from the solarium. I shudder and look away, going to the window.

Peeling back the curtain, I glance out into the backyard. He's cut the huge oak tree that used to stand outside my window. It probably needed to be cut. I still remember how those branches would tap against the glass during the storms and looked so much like long, bony fingers. It scared the hell out of me.

Sitting on the edge of the bed, I slip off my robe and boots and lie down. I pull the blanket up. Reaching over, I turn out the light beside the bed and stare up at the ceiling. I wonder what's happening to Damian, wonder where he is. Wonder if he's safe.

And as my eyelids begin to close, I wonder what would happen to me if he wasn't. If it would free me.

If it's what I want.

Because I keep hearing his words in my head. He loves me. He won't let me go. And all I can think is I need him to call me. To let me know he's okay.

Because if he's not, I don't think I will be either.

27

DAMIAN

"It was a mistake to let him go," Tobias says.

"I fucking heard you the first time and I don't need to hear it again. What I need to know is where the fuck he is."

My brother put on the best show of his life. I have to admit, he's good. He had me fooled and I've never thought myself easily fooled.

What had he said, though? That most men are gullible.

Well, I guess he's right. And hell, maybe he was trying to warn me all along.

"Where the fuck is he?" I demand, because this time I am going to fucking kill him. It's what I should have done instead of letting him off without punishment. What he's done will cost me.

I'm sure my enemies are raising their glasses in a

toast as I stand here and watch my fucking fleet burn down.

"Genoa's under control," Tobias says. "They managed to deactivate all but one of the explosives."

Bombs.

Fucking bombs.

I guess he went old school too.

Clementi has disappeared. Father and sons vanished. That fucker was playing me. Adam Valentina was on his way to disappearing, but my men picked him up at his ex-wife's house. His weakness is his kids. Or maybe it's his wife. Predictable.

The thought bothers me. My brother's words coming back to me bother me.

Cristina is my weakness. He knows it. They all do.

Another explosion draws my attention back to the TV. I wonder if my father is watching my downfall on the news.

A text message vibrates the phone in my palm. I shift my attention to it. Lucas's name pops up on the screen. It's a text. A single word text.

Lucas: Seriously?

I'm about to reply and ask what the fuck he thinks he's doing when I get a second one.

Lucas: I had no idea you were so sentimental. Tell me, do you love your wife? You never answered my question.

I try to call the number, but it goes directly to voicemail. I try again, same thing, so I send a text.

Me: Where the fuck are you, coward?

Nothing.

No reply.

The checkmark telling me the message is sent pops up on the screen, but the second one to tell me it's been delivered never does. He must have switched off his phone.

Do you love your wife?

My throat goes dry.

I dial Cristina's cell phone, but it just rings and rings. Does she even have it?

I try Joseph. He answers on the first ring.

"Where is she?"

"Upstairs in her room."

"You sure?"

"I just checked on her myself. She's asleep."

I exhale. "All right. Thank you, Joseph." I need to calm down. But how the fuck can I calm down when I'm sitting in a back office of one of my warehouses watching my fucking world burn to the fucking ground.

I had no idea you were so sentimental.

Could Lucas know where she is?

"They're here," Tobias says, moving to open the door.

I look up from the monitors to watch Adam Valentina being dragged into the office, his suit jacket askew and torn in places, shirt dirty, one eye turning black before my eyes.

"There," I say, pointing at a chair and rolling up my sleeves.

Valentina looks at me and I wonder how much he's drunk today. "What do you know about this?" I gesture to the screen.

"I know you overshot your position."

Tobias smacks the side of his head with the butt of his gun.

"No, he's right. I underestimated my enemies."

Valentina grins.

"I have at least three of your men in my custody," I tell him.

"They know the risk when they accept. It's why I pay them what I do."

"Yeah but *you* can't pay them anything. I know my brother bankrolled this operation. Him and the Clementi family."

"They're not your only enemies, Damian. You seem to make them at every turn."

"Don't I know it. Where is he? Where's my fucking brother?"

"How should I know? I'm not his fucking keeper."

I gesture to Tobias who grips a handful of Valentina's hair and forces his head down knocking his forehead into the edge of the desk before pulling it back. One of the soldiers rights the chair that fell over.

Valentina's eyes spin as he's seated again. He's got a good, red gash across his forehead.

"That jar your memory?" I ask.

It takes him a minute to focus his eyes on me.

"You were with him and my wife."

His expression changes a little when I mention Cristina.

"What did he want with her?" I ask.

"Just wanted to fuck with you. Where is she? I hope you have her somewhere safe."

"Do you care? What if I told you she was on one of those ships?"

"She wouldn't be. And yeah, I do care. I take offense that you ask."

"Because if she's out of the way, the foundation becomes yours. Free and clear."

"And you think I'd hurt my niece for that?"

"Wouldn't you? You've used her for money before. Pretty easily if I recall."

He's quiet.

"Tell me what he wanted with her."

When he doesn't speak, Tobias grips his hair again, tugging him out of his seat. That same spot on his forehead slams against the desk louder this time.

"Again," I say to Tobias.

"Wait!" Valentina screams as blood runs down into his eyes.

I step closer, then lean down so I'm in his face. "I'm not a very patient man. Tell me what the fuck he wanted in your next breath, or I'll break your fucking face."

"Leverage!"

"What kind of leverage?"

"Get him off me," he says.

"Right after you answer my questions. What kind of leverage?"

"He won't hurt her. He gave me his word."

A pit forms in my gut.

"What the hell do you mean?"

"I helped him because he said he'd get her away from you. He promised not to hurt her."

"Away from me how?"

"Get your goon off me."

"If you won't answer me, you're no use to me. Start with his face and work your way down," I say to Tobias, picking up my coat to walk away. "Go slow."

"Wait!"

I turn back and look at him.

He's on his feet, two men holding him by either arm. "He wanted to be able to track her. In case he needed access to her."

That pit in my stomach turns into a cement block.

"What do you mean, track her? Track her how?"

My brain races to her arm. To how it felt like

there was something hard under the skin. She'd said she thought it was a bite.

"He told her about your scheme to get her pregnant, use the baby to steal the foundation out from under her."

Hearing it like this, spoken out loud, it makes me sound exactly like the monster I warned her about.

I wouldn't have gone through with it, though. I couldn't do that to her. I decided that soon after coming up with the idea.

"He took her to a doctor to give her a birth control shot so it wouldn't work."

My brain rattles with rage.

"He did what?"

"While she was getting that shot, a tracker was inserted."

Tobias is already dialing Joseph when my phone dings again.

Lucas: Okay wait. I should ask my question differently. Maybe then you'll tell me. Because I think I can guess the answer. So maybe a better question is how much? How much do you love your wife, Brother?

CRISTINA

I wake to the distant sound of glass breaking. Disoriented, I rub my eyes and look across the room toward the empty bed as the fog clears my brain.

Scott's bed.

Remembering where I am and why, I sit up.

The blanket falls away and I'm surprised that I fell asleep so quickly. So easily.

I don't know what time it is because there isn't a clock in here, but it's still dark out. I hear footsteps outside my door and swing my legs over the bed.

It must be Damian come for me.

The door opens as I stand up. A man steps into the room.

"In here," he says.

Dark forms move in the direction of my

bedroom. Two. I recognize one and it sends a shiver along my spine.

Because it's not Damian.

"There she is," Lucas says in that tone of his, the one that sounds like we're old friends. The mocking one.

I swallow and back up a step but knock into the nightstand.

"What are you doing here? How did you know I was here?"

His eyes scan me, and I remember what I'm wearing. A little tank top nightie that doesn't hide much.

"My brother sent me to get you. Bring you to him," he says, meeting my eyes again.

I study him but can't read his expression.

He steps deeper into the room until he's only a step from me.

"Where's Joseph?" I ask.

"Downstairs." He looks me over again. "You were sleeping."

I look down too, cross my arms in front of myself before meeting his eyes again. He's too close. I lean back only to feel the lamp at my shoulders. I'm out of space.

"I want to call him," I say when I see the phone in his hand. "I want to call Damian."

He shrugs a shoulder. "Sorry, it's out of charge." He puts it into his pocket. "My brother has all the luck," he says. It's quiet for a long minute while he watches me, wiping something from the corner of his mouth with his thumb, eyes narrowing slightly like he's thinking. Planning. If he comes even a centimeter closer, we'll be touching.

My heart races because he's not here to take me to Damian. I know that.

"You don't scream at the sight of me anymore. Why not?"

I want to tell him it's because the outside isn't nearly as scary as the inside, but panic is setting in. This is bad. Very bad. I feel it in my gut.

He cocks his head and I feel one hand span my lower back. He tugs me to him.

I yelp, hands flying to his chest. He's big, like Damian. And he proved how much stronger than me he is at my uncle's apartment.

"Lucas—"

"Tell me why you don't scream."

"Please."

"Tell me."

"Get off me."

"Why does my brother get to have everything he wants, and I get stuck with this face? Because I admit, I want the pretty girl too."

"The rules say you can't touch—"

He snorts. "You think I give a fuck about any rules."

"Let me go!"

"Boss," someone says behind us.

"Yeah." Lucas doesn't turn.

"It's all set to go."

"You mean to blow," Lucas says with a strange look. The man only chuckles. "Get out and close the door. I need a minute with my sister-in-law."

Without a word, he's gone, and the door closes behind him.

"Get on the bed," Lucas says, releasing me.

"What?"

"Get on the bed."

"Why?"

"Because I said so."

"Lucas—"

"Get on the goddamned bed!"

His tone is so sharp that without a thought, I drop to the edge of the bed.

He looks down at me and I try to not look away from him. I try not to look at his crotch, which is at eye level.

"Put your feet up."

"What?"

"Your feet on the bed. Pull your feet up on the bed."

I do, setting my knees between us, but it's clearly not what he wants because he grips them and forces them apart, pushing me back onto my elbows when he does. My nightie rides up to my belly and he keeps hold of me, looking at me. At my spread legs. Between them.

He swallows, and I make the mistake of looking at his crotch expecting to find him erect. I'm surprised when I don't.

"Lucas—"

"Damian would kill me if I touched you, isn't that right?" he asks, dragging his gaze to mine. "His." He says that last word with disgust and shakes his head. "When you should be mine." He pushes my legs closed and stands looming over me, studying me. "If things were the way they were meant to be, if I were your master and not my brother, would you kiss me?"

"What?"

"Or would you close your eyes so you wouldn't have to see me every time I came near you?"

Something about the way he says it makes me stop and I remember how people looked at me after Scott and Mom died. I remember that pity. And what I see in his eyes is exactly how I felt whenever I'd look at any of them.

I try to wipe the pity from my expression. It's a powerful thing, that. It can make a victim or a villain out of you. I know what it's made of Lucas and I need to be very careful with him.

"What happened to you is terrible, but it doesn't have to define you now. It doesn't have to be the way it is between you and Damian. He loves you. He misses you."

A moment of confusion creases his forehead, then he grins. "We're way past psychoanalysis, sweetheart. Just answer my question."

"You don't want me, Lucas. You want to take what's his. That's what this is about. That's all any of this has ever been about for you."

He sighs, grins. "True that I want to take what's his, but don't underestimate yourself, sweetheart." He shifts his grip to my arm and hauls me up. "I have one more surprise for my brother tonight," he says as he drags me through my room and out the door.

"What are you doing?"

He doesn't answer me as he forces me through the hallway and down the stairs.

"Everyone out!" he calls to the soldiers scattered on the first floor.

They begin to file out as we descend. As I take in the smell. Register what it is.

Gasoline.

Gallons and gallons of gasoline on their sides and emptied all over the living and dining rooms. Soaking our furniture and carpets, my mom's favorite curtains.

"Lucas, what are you doing? Let me go!" I scream as I miss a step and he has to catch me before I go flying face-first down the rest of the stairs.

"I told you I have a surprise for my dear brother."

I can guess what that surprise is. I smell it. Gasoline fills my nostrils, making me nauseous.

"No, Lucas…"

I watch his men file out of the front door. I see Joseph and the other two lying on the ground, one in the foyer, shot between the eyebrows. Joseph is still alive but barely conscious as he bleeds out and the other face down in the corner of the living room.

"You can't leave them…you have to get them help!"

He just snorts.

The front window is smashed. That must have been the shattering glass I heard.

"Let me go!" I cry out, fighting with all I have as he drags me through the dining room and down the hall, past the photos I'd been looking at just hours earlier.

He doesn't let me go. He just keeps walking and his grip is like a vise around my arm. For the second time tonight, I pass by our happy, smiling faces as he takes me toward my father's study door.

"Lucas, please!" He opens the door and drags me in, then closes it behind us. "No!"

"Sit," he says, pushing me into my father's desk chair.

At least the smell isn't as bad in here. I don't see any empty canisters either.

"What are you doing?" He picks up a length of rope that he'd set on a chair and a flashback to that night eight years ago makes the scream catch in my throat. "Lucas?"

He doesn't speak. Instead, he slips the loop around my neck.

Instinctively, I reach up for it, but he's too strong and easily pulls it tight, forcing my head backward. He looks down at me and I see myself reflected in his eyes, eyes and mouth wide in shock and terror.

He grins and loosens the rope a little.

"Don't worry, it's not the same noose my father used to hang yours." He gets to work, slinging it over the beam above my head.

"What are you doing?" Terror like I've never felt before grips me as I close both hands around the rope at my neck trying to give myself room to breathe.

He swings it again and tugs, and I'm up on my feet when he does.

"Lucas!"

"Relax. We have a little time yet," he says, securing the rope somewhere behind me and coming to stand in front of me.

I'm up on my tiptoes and the breaths I manage to take are labored, painful. I'm barefoot, I remember, feeling the rough carpet beneath my toes. I didn't have a chance to put my boots on.

He sits on the edge of the desk and looks up at me, cocking his head to the side, grinning like the fucking Joker himself.

"Answer my question, will you? Would you kiss me or turn your head if it were me and not—"

"Damian," I choke out, cutting him off. Pissing him off.

He gets up and walks away. "Is on his way. Unless he's a complete idiot, which honestly, he could be." He's back in front of me again. "Don't worry, we'll wait for him." He leans toward me. "I wonder…" He trails off and pokes his finger in my belly, pushing me off balance.

I try to reach up for the rope as the noose tightens when gravity takes control, and for the first time in my life, I know—really know—how terrified my father must have been. I know how he must have felt in those final moments.

No, not moments.

Minutes.

Benedict Di Santo dragged them out.

"Gotcha," he says, catching me. "Let's take a selfie for my brother."

I'm trying to get my hands back around the noose, trying to loosen it when the flash blinds me.

"Aww," he says, checking the photo. He vacillates between madness and rage, and I'm not sure which is scarier. "You weren't smiling. But I guess it'll have to do."

He hits send on the image, and it's not even a second later that his phone dings with a message, then rings and rings and rings. Lucas finally shuts it off and sends it flying against the far wall, shattering it.

"He's on his way," he says to me more calmly, that rage sounding like it's in check, but I know better. "We should get you ready."

He grabs me by the waist, pulls me close, then sets me on my knees on my father's chair.

"Please don't do this. You don't want to do this."

He jerks me once. "How do you know what I want?"

"I don't. I don't, but I know what Damian wants. He told me. He told me everything."

He doesn't speak, but his eyes grow intent on mine.

"He doesn't blame you. He loves you. And he wants you back. The way you two were."

He snorts, but in his eyes, I swear I see a flash of someone different. Someone younger. Someone afraid. And I know he wants to believe me.

"He told me you were born holding hands. Your father poisoned you against each other, but it doesn't have to be like that. Not anymore."

Dark eyes search mine and I wonder if I've gotten through. If this is salvageable. But then a moment later, he chuckles.

"You know what's really funny? And sad, actually. I think you really believe all that. I think he does too." He tugs me close again, so close I feel his warm breath on my face when he speaks. "The thing is, I don't want it. I don't want any of it. Besides, he had a chance to stop all of this. He had a chance to put me out of my misery and to save you and you know what he chose? To save himself. He didn't choose you and he didn't choose me. He chose to save himself from a lifetime of guilt. Now get up."

He lets me go and I shrink back, kneeling on my father's chair. I remember how big it used to look to me. His favorite chair. Worn leather. The scent of the cigars he liked to smoke in here still clinging to the leather beneath that of the gasoline slowly creeping in here.

"I'd kiss you!" I cry out, desperate to stop this. I twist around so I can see him. He's moved behind me, but the words come out choked because he's tightening the rope.

He pauses. "Would you?"

"I would because you're not a monster. I know it. I see it."

He cocks his head, considers. "Really?"

I don't understand. I can't read him.

"I think you need glasses then," he adds and starts to pull the rope.

I try to scream, but I can't. I look up to watch the length of it move through the beam. Tears stream down my face as I stand, the chair moving beneath me on its wheels.

He's going to hang me.

He's going to hang me like his father hanged my father.

The chair stills.

"I got you, sweetheart."

Sweetheart.

I try to drag in a breath.

"Don't worry. Get on your feet now. Up. That's it."

I can breathe. There's some slack in the rope. But as soon as I'm on my feet, he tightens it again, and that slack is gone, and I'm on tiptoe again.

If he moves, if he lets the chair go, I'm dead.

I look down at him and he looks up at me.

"You don't want this," I say, words choked.

"No, you're right. I don't want it for you. But I can't let you go. Don't you see? It has to end. And you're the sacrifice. One way or another, you were always going to be the sacrifice. I'm sorry, Cristina."

I think it's the first authentic thing he's said to me. And behind the madman, I see him again. I see that boy. The scared, hurt little boy.

But I also know it's too late. Too late for him. Too late for me.

That's when I hear commotion coming from outside

"There he is," Lucas says, the Joker-like tone back, the madman. He switches the monitor on my father's desk on. We watch the men gathered outside. Tobias and Damian walk to the front door and open it.

I'm surprised Lucas's men are gone.

"Leave your weapons at the door," he yells loudly. "And you come in alone, Brother. Alone or she swings," he calls out. "I'm watching." He's behind me keeping the chair from rolling.

"I'm coming alone. Do not hurt her."

"Aww. He does care," Lucas says to me, making a face that makes me want to punch him or kick my foot into his nose. But if I do either, I'm dead. He lets go of that chair and I will swing.

The door opens a moment later and I take in Damian's face, his eyes, as he sees me. As he sees the only reason I'm not dead is because his brother has his foot on the leg of the chair so it doesn't slip out from under me.

"Cut her down and let her go." He sounds calm, but I hear the tension in his voice. I'm learning Damian. "She has absolutely nothing to do with this."

I want to tell him to run. To get out. It's a trap. He must know it. He must smell the gasoline. Lucas is going to kill him. He's going to kill us all. But every breath is torture, and it's taking all I have to remain as still as possible.

"Don't move, Cristina," Damian tells me. He must see my struggle.

"When did you buy the house? I had no idea," Lucas asks.

"Let her go, Lucas. I'm here. You have what you want."

"No, not really. Actually, I don't have anything I want."

"Then tell me what the hell it is. Tell me and I'll give it to you!"

Lucas stops, and I see the change in expression, like something's dawning on him. And then I see that grin, the Joker-like one.

"You already are, Brother. Everything ends tonight. We all end tonight."

I hear it before I smell it. A whoosh.

Fire.

Fire catching.

Fire racing to devour the gasoline.

Damian takes two urgent steps closer.

"Stay where you are. You come closer, and I let go of the chair."

Damian puts his hands up and stops.

"You have to admit, it will be a poetic end, don't you think? Everything back to where it all started. Sorta. I mean, I can't take you back to the train tracks, but she hangs like her father did. Like she should have eight years ago. And you and me and Father, we all burn. Like we should have. But only after you watch her die."

"You are not this person, Lucas," Damian says.

Do I feel the heat of the fire already? Is that possible? I hear it coming closer. It's raging.

"I'm exactly this person, Damian. Dad was right to choose me. I am what he wanted. I am exactly that. He must have seen it, too. Recognized himself in me."

"You're not like him."

"I'm more like him than you'll ever let yourself believe."

"She's innocent. Let her go. I'll burn. If that's what you want, I'll burn. I don't care. Let her go before it's too late."

"There's the answer I was looking for. My brother's in love." Lucas turns his face up to mine. "Isn't it sweet? He loves you. If you had any doubt, now you know. He'll die for you. That's the truest test, isn't it? He wouldn't die for me or for his sister or his mother, but he'll die for you."

Damian lunges for him then.

I would scream if I could as something explodes inside the house, and when the study door blows open, I feel the enormous heat of the fire on my face.

I see Damian's hands around his brother's throat, know the moment they go down because that's the instant the chair rolls out from under me.

My feet race to find purchase, but there's nothing beneath me, only air. I claw at the rope at my neck, but I can't get under it. I'm choking, slowly strangling.

Is this how they did it to my father? That's what he'd said, isn't it? Benedict Di Santo had choked him slowly. Only snapped his neck after he'd had his fun.

Fire licks the walls, devouring wood. The drapes along the windows catch, and I'm fighting, spinning, and they're still on the ground. My arms fall away as I wheeze the tiniest breath in.

Not enough, though. Not enough.

I feel myself slip away. As I stop fighting, my legs twitching as I take in my last smoke-filled gasp of breath and hang.

29

DAMIAN

"You goddamn piece of shit!" I charge my brother, slamming him hard against the back wall.

Glass shatters in the other room, exploding in the fire.

"She has nothing to do with this. Nothing. This is you and me!" He doesn't fight me, not right away. He's laughing. He's fucking laughing the laugh of a lunatic.

I hear her behind me, hear her gasps and choked attempts at breath, hear her terror. I force myself to focus, force myself to look at my brother who's gripping me hard around the collar.

He won't let go.

This is his revenge.

Because even if I don't know who he is, he knows who I am. And he knows my weakness. He wasn't fucking with me when he taunted me about Cristina.

All these years, I've felt sorry for him. He was my father's pawn. Manipulated. Used. The sensitive one. The one I needed to protect even as he pummeled me with his fists. How has he become this person? This monster?

He's got me by the collar. Even though I've thrown enough punches to see blood on his lip and the beginnings of swelling on his eye, he hasn't hit me. Not once.

"Watch," he says when I stop.

I hear her. She's choking. Dying.

I look up to see her, see her struggle, watch her kick.

I promised to protect her. To keep her safe.

Lucas doesn't let go and I realize that broken sound, it's not her. It's me.

I can't save them both. I have to choose. Tobias was right. It was a mistake letting Lucas live. And my mistake, my weakness, will cost Cristina her life.

Rage hotter than the fire that's swallowing this house burns inside me. I turn, breaking free from Lucas's grip.

Everything happens for a reason, I think.

Nothing is left to chance. Everything comes full circle.

He's fighting me now. He'll do anything to keep me from her. His eyes are locked on mine. As the fire burns nearer, my hand and torso throb, remembering the pain of the last time.

Does Lucas remember?

God. I can still hear his screams that night. I'd forgotten that part. Fire and smoke and burning flesh and a man's screams.

He fights hard—we're well matched—all while my Cristina swings.

But I have something he's not expecting.

I reach into my pocket and take out the switchblade I confiscated from her earlier this evening. The one Lucas made and Michela gave to my wife to protect herself from me.

Ironic what I will use it to do.

I open it.

I don't wait or think or consider. With the hilt in my hand, I do what I should have done at the strip club. I do what my brother asked me to do. Was he too weak to do it himself? Or is this a part of his vengeance? Will he take a part of me to the grave with him?

Flesh gives easily against the sharp blade. It's a feeling I'll never forget. But it's not done. And I keep pushing.

Only when I've buried the length of it in his stomach do I stop.

Only then does everything stop.

He rounds his back, looks down between us, looks at the dagger in my grip, the blade buried inside him. It's like he just realizes what's happened. What I've done.

He looks at the circle of blood on his shirt, on mine, on my hands.

Blood. Warm blood.

Always blood with me.

Annabel's blood.

Michela's blood.

Cristina's.

My dying brother's.

It's all on my hands.

Lucas looks up, meets my eyes, and I see pain. Old pain. New pain.

I don't see fear, though. That's gone. Maybe he was ready all along. Maybe I was wrong about having seen fear last night.

His hands go from my shoulders to my face, then down to close over my hands. I think he wants to pull it out, but he doesn't.

Keeping his eyes on mine and with a choked grunt, he tugs it sharply upward.

He watches me, eyes dimming, and I think he wants to say something. I think...fuck...his knees buckle and blood leaks from the corner of his mouth. Still, his hands grip mine, grip that knife.

He's slipping away. And I have to let him go.

I pull the dagger out. Release him. Let him drop. Knife in my hand, I let my brother go.

And I know the moment his soul leaves his body.

I feel it. I feel my twin die because something inside me lets go, too.

But then from the corner of my eye I see her stop moving. Stop fighting.

No.

Not again. I can't walk away again when they all die around me.

I won't.

As if in some time warp, I turn to look up at her. Her eyes meet mine for an instant. A fading, dimmed violet haze as her body twists, dangling from the rope. Arms dropping to her sides. Her right leg twitching once more just before her eyes close.

The fire sends hot smoke in my direction, making me choke as I leap onto the desk and gather Cristina's limp body to mine. I hold her, give her some slack as I use the bloodied knife to cut her down.

Fire licks up my back.

My god, the pain.

How can there be so much pain?

I keep the knife in my hand and hold her to me, cradling her head against me. Her arms and legs hang loose, her body boneless. I don't look back. I don't think. I step over my dead brother, then turn my back into the window and throw myself through it. It's the only way to protect her as shards rip my back. I land hard, the impact knocking the wind from me.

Turning, I lay her down and look at her.

"Please don't be dead. Please don't be dead." No more blood on my hands.

Not your blood on my hands.

Touching her face, I put my head on her chest to try to hear over the groans of the house, over the bellowing of the fire. But I can't hear, and her chest is still. I smear my brother's blood on her face as I try to rouse her. It's on her mouth, her too delicate hands and wrists.

"Breathe. Breathe. Hate me but breathe."

But she doesn't. She won't move and when I lift her hand, it just drops down to her stomach when I let it go. Rope still dangles from her neck. It's done. What my father wanted. Too soon, though. She didn't get that year Annabel had.

Dead.

No.

No, no, no.

Please. Fuck. No.

"Damian!" Tobias screams in the distance. I don't look up. I don't care.

"I'll let you go," I whisper close to her ear. "Just breathe. Just breathe."

"Fuck! We need to move!" He's closer.

Something crackles and bursts behind me. I smell burnt meat and feel the brand of an iron on my shoulder. But I don't care. I don't care about any of it.

"Just open your eyes and I'll let you go. I promise."

"Damian!" Arms pull at me. "Leave her. She's gone. The fucking house is coming down!"

And as he says it, a beam big and heavy flies through the sky, flames like wings as it lands too close.

I get to my feet, but I don't go when Tobias tries to drag me. I bend to lift her body. Limp, dead weight, she hangs over my shoulder like a ragdoll as I run.

An ungodly sound deafens us. When I look back, I watch the house topple, watch what's left of it disappear into the flames, my brother's dead body in its belly. His flesh soon to be ash. Dust.

Dead.

Like he wanted.

For a long moment, I can't see through the thick smoke. Through the debris and dust.

I shift my grip on Cristina and drop to my knees on the ground. I lay her on her back, and even now, even in death, all I can think is how beautiful she is. How innocent. How she didn't deserve any of this.

I push hair from her temple, but when I try to wipe the ash from her face, I smear blood along her cheek instead. I kiss her forehead, her cheeks, her mouth. I think about how Lucas was right in his prediction. I break everything I touch. And she's broken beyond repair.

"I love you," I whisper in her ear. Apart from Annabel and my mother, I'd never said those words to anyone before Cristina. "And I'm sorry."

A sadness like I've never felt twists inside my chest.

I wonder why people say they loved someone in the past tense when that person dies. Do they stop loving them then? Is that what happens? How conditional their love.

"I love you." Present tense. "Do you hear me? Do you fucking hear me!" I shake her. Hurting her still. Even now.

Blood on my hands again. Always blood with me.

When I loosen the rope from around her neck, I notice how it cut into her skin. I pull it over her head, but before I can lean down to kiss her lips again, before I can whisper again that I love her, her body jerks violently. Her eyes fly open as she gasps for breath, hands to her neck, desperate for air.

She opens her mouth and I think she would scream if she could, but she can't get enough air in.

Another choked sound. Me this time.

She clutches at me, hands falling away, grasping at nothing. I lift her to sit as she wheezes not believing my eyes. Not believing this miracle.

She's alive.

Cristina is alive.

Her hand closes around my forearm and pain makes me hiss.

I look down at it, beneath her hand is the raw, red skin burned anew. Freshly charred flesh. The smell is mixed in with all the rest of them.

But even through the pain all I can do is look at her and hold her to me. And I remember what I promised her just now. What I said I'd do if she'd only breathe. If she'd just open her eyes and take one more breath.

30

CRISTINA

"*Just open your eyes and I'll let you go.*"

I do as he says and open my eyes to see Damian standing over my bed. I blink, sitting up.

"Hey," I say, touching my hair to smooth it, wondering what I look like in my hospital gown while he's standing there in a dark suit looking as impeccable as ever. Apart from a bruise on the side of his jaw, stitched cuts on his face, and the bandage around his hand and arm, he looks the same.

There are more bandages underneath the clothes, though. And he's not quite the same. There's a little more gray in the five o'clock shadow and along his temples. And as put together as he is I know the exterior masks the depth of the loss he's feeling.

He killed his brother. His twin brother. Even if

Lucas was crazy, even if Damian had no choice, he still pushed the knife into his brother's belly and felt the blood spill from him.

And this is a man who has kept his emotions hidden for years. For all his life, probably. A man used to being on his own. Alone. Always alone.

The thought is unsettling. I don't like it.

It's been six days since the night our world collapsed around us. Crashed down onto us in a fire built of rage and fury and despair and too much hate.

"Hey." He doesn't smile. I see how his gaze darkens as it moves from the bandage on my arm to where they removed the tracker and finally to my neck. I know it's bruised. I've seen it. Can feel how tender it is.

"Are they releasing you?" I ask, surprised. I thought I'd be out earlier than him.

"I've released myself." The emotion I just saw is gone, masked. Shuttered. Shutting me out.

"What?"

"I have to take care of some things. How are you feeling?"

I shrug a shoulder, something heavy settling in the pit of my stomach. "I'm okay. Sit down."

"I can't stay."

A lump forms in my throat. Swallowing it is harder than I imagine it should be. "What do you mean you can't stay?"

I stare up at his closed-off eyes. They give nothing away.

He sets a large envelope on the table beside the bed.

"What's that?"

"My promise."

I look from the envelope to him. "What do you mean?"

"I'm sorry for what he did to you. For what happened to you because of me."

"Damian, that wasn't—"

"I'm sorry I couldn't protect you like I promised but…" He gestures to the envelope. "I can keep one promise."

"What are you talking about?"

"You can stay at the penthouse as long as you need. Details are in the envelope. Everything is taken care of. You don't have to worry about anything."

"Damian, I don't—"

"I need to go." He checks his watch.

When he takes a step away, I sit upright and push the blanket from me. "Where?"

He comes back to me, sits on the edge of the bed, and softly brushes hair back from my face. He gives me a sad smile.

"I'm finally doing what's best for you. What's really best for you. It's the first unselfish thing I've done when it comes to you."

He leans closer and I see is the sadness in his eyes. It runs deep. An abyss of it. And I feel the cracking of my heart.

I open my mouth to say his name, to tell him I understand. To say anything at all. But he cups the back of my head and presses his lips to my forehead.

Closing my eyes, I place my hand on his cheek as a tear slips down my face.

This is his goodbye. I know it.

He draws back, hand still on the back of my head. He looks at me for a long minute. And what I see in his eyes breaks my heart in two.

Regret. Sadness. Too much of it.

And me on the outside.

31

DAMIAN

I need to keep my promise. I need to do one right thing.

And as hard as it is, walking away is the only way to do that. But it takes all I have to follow through.

I get up and walk out of the room. Closing that door behind me feels like I'm leaving a piece of myself behind. I think it's my heart.

Coward.

Tobias falls into step beside me as we make our way out of the hospital.

"I have two of our best soldiers guarding her. She'll be fine."

I nod, not trusting myself to speak.

My promise to her, is it a lie? A selfish lie told only to protect myself?

"The Clementis are at the warehouse," Tobias continues.

Business. I have to get to the business of my revenge. Show my enemies what happens when you cross me.

"Good," I say, sounding a little harder as I feel the familiar stone walls erect themselves around me. As hard as it is, as painful, I have to keep thoughts of the way I found her at the forefront of my mind. Keep the image of her with that rope around her neck burned on my brain. Feel the weight of her limp body in my arms as I carried her out of that house.

I don't have to work hard to remember the sensation of my heart twisting when I'd thought I was too late. When I'd thought she was gone.

And I can't think about how she looks in that bed in the other room. Small and vulnerable and sad. I just have to remember the angry bruises around her throat and be grateful that Lucas was wrong. That I didn't break her. At least not so much that she couldn't be put back together again.

This is better for her. Safer. I need to let her go because nothing changes with Lucas gone. My business will be rebuilt. My enemies will not lessen.

This is best for her.

Coward.

"You sure about Valentina?"

Tobias has a very clear black and white outlook

on life. You betray me, you die. Period. No second chances. Not reprieves.

He was right about Lucas. My letting him walk away without punishment led to this. Led to a destruction I didn't imagine him capable of. So yeah, I understand Tobias.

But Valentina is her family. And that's about the only thing that's saving his life. I'll be watching him, though. He goes within a few miles of her, and I will fucking kill him.

"He's been dealt with." He's in the hospital somewhere too with two broken legs, a dislocated shoulder, and several busted ribs. "For now." He knows he'll be receiving another beating once he heals just to drive the message home.

Lucas's plan succeeded, at least in part. Most of my ships are destroyed. Lucas, with the help of the Clementi family and Cristina's uncle, accomplished that. That I can deal with. I've rebuilt out of nothing before. I can do it again.

But that's not the worst of it.

In the study, I was too focused on Cristina and the fire and my insane brother to process what he'd said. Just a few words that I missed.

"...you and I and Father, we all burn. Like we should have."

"My sister and Bennie?" I ask.

"Safe and sound. They're staying in California

until arrangements are made for your brother. Not your father, though."

I nod. I understand.

The explosives weren't only set at the shipping yards, and Cristina's family's home wasn't the only one my brother burned to the ground.

The house Upstate is mostly gone. Lucas arranged for that, too. And my father went down with it. Strangely, the only wing that survived was Lucas's.

"I can take care of the Clementis," Tobias offers when we exit the hospital.

Three dark SUVs pull up and I walk to the second one. I open the back door and turn to him.

"I have no doubt, but I'll be dealing with them myself. Especially the old man."

We climb into the SUV and it takes all I have not to look back at the building inside which my wife, my soon to be ex-wife, lies.

I shift my gaze to my hands instead, peeling off my wedding band. Without a word, I drop it into my pocket, the one closest to my heart. The one inside which hers sits.

32

CRISTINA

Five Months Later

The house is gone. Everything inside it destroyed. With all the gasoline Lucas had used to fuel his hate, he wiped out every last remnant of my family. Every single memory of us.

We were happy once, all of us. Happy in our home.

I look up at the treehouse. That survived, at least.

Five months have passed since the fire, but I swear I can still smell the smoke while standing in the cleared lot.

Damian lost his ships and his house Upstate. His

father is dead. Burned in the fire. Lucas killed him, too. At least Michela and her son are safe.

I know the only reason my uncle is still alive is because of me, because he is my uncle and Liam and Simona's father. No matter what kind of man he is, I know losing him would devastate them.

When I was discharged, I went to see him. He could barely speak he was so heavily medicated, but I needed to see him. I had one question to ask him and after he answered it, I needed him to know that I didn't forgive him. I was finished being manipulated and used by him.

He knew Lucas had the doctor insert that tracker in my arm and did nothing to stop it. Did he know what Lucas intended to do to me? He said no when I asked him. Said he'd never have gone along with that.

I'm honestly not sure I believe him.

I don't feel sorry for him or the shape he's in. I'm not really sure what that says about me, but I've buried my head for so long I just can't anymore. If this is who I am, a woman who knows right from wrong, who understands that blood doesn't exempt one from betrayal and looks with eyes wide open on the violence done to a man and doesn't feel remorse, then that is who I am.

I was young when this started, a child when my uncle took me into his home. He used me. He used me all my life, and even as I got older, even as questions came, I never asked them. I accepted the life I was given. Even the roses that arrived like clockwork on my birthday. I never asked. I stole the notes and the ribbons out of the trashcan and never asked why someone hated me enough to send me dead flowers to mark each passing year. Never asked about the men who were in my house the night of my father's murder.

I was too afraid of so many things but mostly of losing him too. Him and Liam and Simona.

After the accident, I'd been alone, really. My father was dealing with his own guilt, his own pain at the loss of them, and he couldn't take care of me, too. He couldn't take my pain. I understand it.

But I'm done walking through my life with my head down. I'm finished being weak.

Inside the envelope Damian left that day were divorce papers. He'd already signed his name. The settlement is a very generous one. I'd be stupid not to take it.

Along with that was the deed to this ruined house. The land. Damian signed it all over to me contingent on the divorce. I don't know what I'll do with it, though. I don't want to rebuild here. I don't want to be here. Not now. But I also can't leave New York City. It's where Damian is, even though I haven't seen him once. It's where I feel closest to him.

I haven't gone back to school, although the

semester started several weeks ago. Everything just feels so different. So much less important.

Liam thinks I should see a therapist to talk about it all, but I don't want that. I guess in a way, I want to keep a little part of Damian inside me. A piece of him for myself now that he's gone. Disappeared from my life.

I guess he let me go like he promised.

I touch the spot where my wedding ring was for the hundredth time. Even though I only wore his ring for days, it feels strange not to have it, not to feel the weight of it on my finger. It never occurred to me I'd miss it.

Miss him.

Giving a shake of my head, I walk toward the treehouse. It'll be dark soon, but I've put this off too long.

Dusk has turned the sky a deep, somber blue. It fits.

I reach the base of the tree. It's singed but the firefighters managed to save it. I stand on tiptoe to reach the rope ladder that's tucked on a branch. I jump to try to get to it, but it's too high. I'm just looking around for something to stand on when I hear footsteps crunch the blackened, dead ground behind me.

With a gasp, I spin, not sure what to expect. A ghost? Another monster? But when I see him, see this union of ghost and monster and man, my heart skips a beat and my breath catches in my throat and I have to try hard to quash the hope that swells inside my chest.

As the last of the sun disappears into the horizon and the moon casts a silvery light over us, I'm sure my face registers a myriad of emotions.

But Damian's expression doesn't change.

I shudder with a sudden chill.

He strides right up to me, extending an arm to release the rope.

I stare up at him. I'd forgotten how tall he is. Forgotten how I feel around him. How my body aches to lean into him. Was it always like this?

We stand like that for a minute. Him just inches from me in his dark suit, hand around the rope. His smell so familiar, making my heartbeat kick up like he used to do.

His eyes are locked on mine and I wonder if he's missed me, too. If he looks over his shoulder for me like I do him.

For a moment, I indulge the thought that maybe he has.

I count the fresh scars on his face, cuts from the glass when he used his body to shield mine. Even for the ruined skin, he's still beautiful. More so.

But I know this isn't the worst of the damage. That's on the inside. I think his heart must be covered over in scar tissue.

"You haven't signed the papers," he says. I

remember now how deep his voice is, how it seems to vibrate right inside me.

It takes me a moment to find my voice. "You disappeared."

He literally vanished off the face of the earth. It was impossible to get in touch with him. I even drove to the house Upstate, but that was a waste of time. It was locked up so tight and under such heavy guard, I couldn't get past the gate.

"That was the point. You haven't signed, Cristina. I can't keep my promise if you don't sign."

"How did you know I was here?"

"You also haven't been back to school. The semester started. Why aren't you at school?"

"How—"

"Why?"

"Are you having me followed?"

"For your safety. I still have enemies and you're still my wife."

I raise my eyebrows. "Are you doing that—having me followed—*for my own good*?" I ask, suddenly angry. "Like when you walked out of that hospital room before we could even talk about anything?" I hadn't even known about my uncle being there too until Liam told me. And the whole hanging experience, it still gives me nightmares. I wake up feeling like I'm choking to this day.

His jaw tenses, and his hand around the rope

tightens, making his bicep flex and the suit jacket hug his arm.

"You just left me there to process it all on my own. To try to make sense of it alone."

"I didn't leave you alone, I—"

"Fuck you. You left me alone. Soldiers don't count. So, fuck you, Damian. Stop having me followed. You walked away and you can just keep walking. We're done."

"Then why haven't you signed the divorce papers?"

I bite the inside of my cheek and glance away momentarily because I don't know. It's what I wanted, to be free. He was giving me what I wanted. All I had to do was sign.

"You almost died, Cristina. I left to protect you."

"No. You left so you wouldn't have to face all the shit. All the messy feelings. Your brother is dead. Have you even talked to anyone about that?"

"Like a shrink?"

"Yeah, like a shrink."

"Didn't realize you were so positive on them. Liam says you refuse to go."

I feel my eyebrows creep way up on my forehead. "You're talking to Liam?"

He clears his throat and shifts his gaze momentarily like he didn't intend on giving that away.

"Since when have you been in contact with my cousin?"

"Cristina—"

"Since when, Damian?"

"I needed to be sure you were all right."

"Well, I'm not all right. And I'll deal with my cousin. You stop talking to him and for the third time, fuck you. Give me that and go away." I try to take hold of the rope ladder, but he tugs it out of reach and chuckles when I jump to try and grab it.

"What's so funny?"

"You."

"I'm done being your plaything."

"You're not my plaything. You were meant to be, but you never were."

That takes me aback, but I force my eyes to narrow. Force myself to feel anger. "I said give me that and go away."

"No."

"You're on my property. I'll call the police."

"It's not your property until you sign the divorce papers."

He's right. "Technicality," I say, jutting my chin out and folding my arms across my chest.

"I don't want you out here on your own, Cristina."

"I'm not yours to worry about anymore. And besides, I'm not on my own. You have men following me, remember? And also, you're here."

"I'm here to talk some sense into you. Or I was."

"You're here to clear your conscience."

He considers for a long minute. "You're right. If you'd done as you were told and signed the papers and moved on with your life, I would have a clearer conscience."

I'm surprised. I guess I thought he'd deny it.

"I've never been good at doing as I'm told. I thought you knew that," I retort.

His gaze sweeps my face, and one corner of his mouth curves upward. He licks his lips and gets a familiar glint in his eyes. It's the one that makes him look dirty.

That makes me feel dirty.

"You know what? I change my mind," he says.

"Change your mind about what?"

He tugs the rope ladder, testing it, then extends it out. "After you."

I drop my arms. "What's your game?"

"No game. Go on."

"You're coming with me?"

"I told you I don't want you out here on your own."

I study his face in the moonlight. "What are you doing, Damian?"

"You know what? I'm giving you a choice."

"What do you mean?"

"Do you want me, Cristina? Because this time you should choose for yourself." He pauses for a long minute. "Do you want me to stay or do you want me to go? Truth." His face is serious again, eyes dark as they study me intently.

Do I want him? That's what he's asking me.

I look down at the ground, then slowly back up at him. That swelling inside me is back and it brings tears to my eyes. God, I missed him. I missed him so much.

But isn't it best to tell him to go?

My hands tremble to touch him for the first time in too long, fingertips just brushing his stomach through his shirt, his chest, feeling the muscle beneath, that strength that feels so good. That feels like home.

I shift my gaze up to his.

Do I want him? Do I want the man who stole me from my life? Who plotted for almost a decade to punish me for the sins of my father?

This man who warned me about monsters when I was just a little girl. This man who was meant to be my monster.

Do I want him?

33

DAMIAN

"I want you," she says.

Relief.

It's like my lungs just opened up and I can breathe again.

Cristina seems different. No, not that. She's more. More herself, maybe. Stronger. She's always had defiance in her, but this is something else.

But I guess almost dying will do that to you.

She takes hold when I extend the ladder to her and starts her climb. It's wobbly and she stops to look down when she's only a few rungs up.

I climb up behind her, put my hands just above hers on the ladder. "I've got you."

She studies me and I wonder if she hears what I'm saying. What I'm really saying. I do have her. And I won't let her fall. Not again. Never again.

"I know," she says, and something shifts inside me. A pain in my chest eases.

We climb in silence, Cristina's body just inches ahead of mine, mine cocooning hers. And it feels good that I should be here. Feels right.

These past months have been different than I expected. Emptier. Or not emptier but empty again. Empty like before the night I took Cristina. The night I forced her into my home and into my life.

I knew walking away would be hard, but I thought throwing myself into the business—into rebuilding—would be enough. Would make it bearable, at least. I missed her, though. Missed her too much. And it's different from how I miss my brother.

Lucas is dead. He died at my hands, his blood drenching them literally and figuratively. I mourn my brother daily. I mourn what happened to us. Why we became what we became. And I still wonder if there had been a chance to save him. Save us. Wonder if I could have done more.

In a way, I think that's one of the reasons Cristina isn't ever far from my mind. I have a chance with her. A chance I never really had with Lucas, not born into the family we were born into.

Once we're to the top, she ducks into the small entrance. She scoots over and I have to twist to get inside. For two kids, I can see how this space would seem big, but I feel like a giant in here. Like Gulliver.

Moonlight pours in through the window cutout.

We both look around. A small child's table rests against one wall.

"We strung a pulley system to lift things from the ground. Scott's idea," she says.

The table is worn, one leg broken. Two chairs sit on either side and games are stacked along the far corner in their damaged boxes.

Christmas lights still drape the crookedly cut out window. They're plastic so I'm sure their best days are about a decade in the past.

"Snacks," she says, opening another cardboard box. I peer inside. It's empty but for plastic wrapping that's been gnawed through. Probably squirrels.

"I came up here once after Mom and Scott died," she says, crawling to the plastic toy oven that has survived these years even though I'm sure the colors were more vibrant before. She opens it and I watch her face, the anticipation turning to relief as she pulls out a little tin trinket box.

"My mom bought it at an antique market. I'd thought it was so ugly. I wanted a Barbie one." She carries it to where I'm sitting.

"What's in it?"

She opens the lid and smiles when she sees the gold locket inside. She lifts it out.

"I'd taken it out of her bedroom on the night Dad and I had come home without the other half of our family."

The gold chain unravels as she palms it.

She opens it, peering at the pictures behind the ovals of glass. A family photo.

"I'd just come home from the hospital in this one," she says. I can see her parents' happy faces, the bundle in her mother's arms that is Cristina, her one-year-old brother tugging at her mom's leg. "Liam was able to get some photos off my uncle's computer but there aren't many."

"May I?"

She hands it to me, and I peer closely, "You really look like her." I hand it back. "I'm sorry you lost it all. That's not how I wanted this to go."

"I know."

A blanket of darkness falls over me. Maybe it's being here where it happened. Maybe it's being near her. I don't know.

"I guess it's fitting he chose fire," I say.

"I'm sorry, Damian. I'm sorry you lost so much. I'm sorry about Lucas. And I'm even sorry about your father." That last part is tacked on after a moment's pause.

She shudders as a cool breeze blows in from the window.

I extend my arm over her shoulder and pull her closer so she's leaning against me.

"They tried to tell me my father wouldn't have suffered. That he was probably asleep. And do you know all I could think? All I hoped? That they were wrong. That he did know what was coming for him. And that he did suffer."

I look at her. I want her to see who I am. What I am. This is the real me. I am a monster. I warned her from day one, and if she stays, she needs to do it with both eyes wide open.

"It's okay. What you feel is okay."

I lean my head back and stare straight ahead, in my periphery I can see her watching me.

"Is it? I'm not really sure about that, sweetheart."

Sweetheart.

It sounds tender. Like how I feel when I think about her. Tender and raw.

"I went there, you know. To find you," she continues.

"I know."

"Will you rebuild the house?" she asks.

"No. At least not yet. I can't sell the land, it has to stay in the family, but I don't want to be there yet. Hell, maybe ever."

"What about Michela? Does she want it?"

"She wants nothing to do with it. She came to Lucas's memorial service but refused to go to our father's. I understand."

"How are you two?" She shifts so I have to look at her.

I touch her cheek to brush hair behind her ear. It's grown a good inch, and her bangs keep falling into her eyes. "We'll be okay," I tell her.

"I'm glad."

I study her. Remember how beautiful her eyes are. Not that I'd forgotten but it's good to see them again. See her again. And not from behind a darkly tinted window or a photograph.

"He told me I'd break you," I say. "Lucas, I mean. He said I break everything I touch. That I'd break you."

"You saved me, Damian. You saved my life."

"You almost died because of me. Because my brother wanted to punish me."

"You saved my life. Period. And I'm not broken."

"No, you're not so easy to break. That's a good thing with me, Cristina."

She leans her head on my shoulder and sighs.

"In the end, he knew me much better than I ever knew him," I say, tucking her closer.

"What do you mean?"

"He asked me if I cared about you. He knew I did. He just wanted to taunt me." I pull back again to look at her. "Why didn't you sign the divorce papers?"

She shifts her gaze.

I touch two fingers to her chin to tilt her face up, so she has to look at me. "Why, Cristina?"

"What you said to me…"

My heartbeat kicks up. I know what she's talking about. When I told her I loved her just before all this happened.

"I heard it and…" She shifts her position so she's sitting up, looking straight into my eyes. "I know it's stupid and I can't explain it. I haven't even told anyone about it because I'm sure even Liam would think I was crazy." She drops her head, shakes it, then pushes her bangs out of her eyes before looking at me. "Did you mean it?"

"When I told you that I love you."

It's not a question but she nods anyway.

"Yes. I meant it. I still do. I love you, Cristina."

"Good. Because I love you, too, Damian."

34

DAMIAN

Studying her in the dim moonlight, I watch the flush creep into her cheeks.

She lowers her lashes to hide her eyes from me, but when she turns away, I take her face in both my hands, making her look at me.

She places her hands over mine, not resisting when I pull her to me.

I close my mouth over hers and kiss her.

This kiss is different than any other. There's no resistance, nothing taken that isn't given. I kiss her and she kisses me.

And when she surrenders to me, I know she's mine. Truly mine for the first time.

EPILOGUE 1
CRISTINA

Four Years Later

I never signed the divorce papers but watched him tuck them away in the safe instead along with our rings.

He wants it to be my choice.

And he doesn't want me to choose just yet.

Given that I turned eighteen the night he took me, I'm okay with that.

It takes me another four years to graduate from college. Damian, Liam, Simona, and their mom attend my graduation. I think I see a man in the distance who resembles my uncle, but I don't tell Damian. And besides, I could be wrong.

In the penthouse, Liam and I are eating cake

while Damian takes my aunt and Simona downstairs to the car waiting to drive them home. They moved back to the city to be closer to Liam who is—or was—still in school here.

I study my cousin as he shoves another forkful of heavily iced chocolate cake into his mouth.

"You still eat like you're growing," I tell him. He's grown than my uncle now and filled out a lot. I see how women look at him whenever we go anywhere. I want to scream that he's only twenty, but I was only eighteen when I fell in love with Damian, so I keep my mouth shut.

"It's good cake. I don't get cake often."

I roll my eyes. "Oh, please. I'm sure any one of your many girlfriends would fall over themselves to bake you a cake if that's what you wanted."

He grins, revealing a dimple in his left cheek under the five o'clock shadow he's perfected.

"They have other uses." He winks to me.

"Don't be gross," I tell him, punching his arm. "And we need to talk."

He shoves more cake into his mouth.

"About school," I add as if he didn't know.

"Here it comes," he mutters under his breath then adds, "Don't be Mom."

"I won't. You don't listen to her."

He shrugs a shoulder and, after finishing his cake, takes my plate and digs into my slice.

"You dropped out of school, Liam."

"I don't need school, Cris. I make a lot of money already."

"But what you're doing isn't safe or legal." He's been honing his hacking skills and he's gotten involved with some questionable people. I only know this because he'd needed to come to Damian for help a little while ago. I'm still not sure Damian would have told me if I hadn't seen Liam when I'd come home earlier than expected from school.

He shifts his gaze to mine, thick lashes around dark eyes. I see why women twice his age fall for him.

"What Damian does is legal? I know more about him than you think."

"This isn't about Damian. This is about you."

"Hey, this is your day. Let's not have this conversation today, okay?"

"Then when? I'm worried about you. I don't want you involved with people like Dad was involved with."

"Then give me the green light to work with Damian."

"No."

"Why not? He could use my skills."

"Is he offering you a job?"

"Are you kidding? He knows you'll kill him if he does."

"Good. He shouldn't. Go back to school. Graduate and get your degree. You know you can do it in half the time it'd take anyone else."

"Cristina," he groans my name, dropping the fork and leaning back, arm over his stomach.

The door opens and Damian walks inside. He takes us in. He doesn't quite agree with me on this one. He sees potential in Liam and that scares me.

Liam checks his watch. "I gotta go." He stands.

"Damian," I urge him with a nod at Liam.

"Sit," Damian tells him. Pulling up a chair in front of us, he turns it around and straddles it as Liam reluctantly drops back into his seat.

He takes an envelope out of his pocket and holds it out to Liam.

"What's that?" Liam asks, eyeing it suspiciously.

"Yeah, what's that?" I parrot.

Liam opens it, skims the sheet, and raises his eyebrows.

"Contract," Damian says, looking at me.

"What kind of contract?" I ask, Liam's growing smile concerning me.

"If he gets his degree in two years, he can have a job with Di Santo International."

"No. No way. He can't work with you—"

Damian holds his hand up, stopping me. "It's legit, Cristina. I won't involve him in anything that isn't."

Liam looks over at me and hands me the contract.

"What have you got to lose?" Damian asks him. "You're twenty years old. You've got plenty of time to find trouble, and I have a feeling it'll come looking for you anyway. This way, I can teach you."

"You mean it? I'll be second in command in Genoa?"

Damian nods.

I look from one to the other and watch as Damian retrieves a pen, holds it out to Liam.

Liam takes it, gives me a happy smile, and signs. As soon as he hands it back to Damian, they both stand. Liam leans down and kisses me on the cheek.

"Don't forget to open my gift later." He winks. He wouldn't let me open it in front of anyone.

"I'm nervous."

He grins, which doesn't ease those nerves. A few minutes later, he's gone, and Damian sits down beside me.

"You bought two years," I say.

"Two years is a start. He'll be fine, Cristina. That kid can take care of himself. Mostly."

"I don't want him to get involved with men like..."

"Men like me," he finishes for me.

I shrug a shoulder.

"He *is* a man like me, sweetheart. And he's an adult. Young, but an adult." He stands and holds out his hand.

I take it and let him pull me to my feet. He tugs me in for a kiss, and instantly, my body reacts, nipples tightening, stomach clenching. I think he's going to lead me into the bedroom, but we go to the study instead.

"What are we doing?" I ask when he closes the door behind us. Leaving me standing at his desk, he walks around it to the safe hidden in a cabinet there. I watch as he crouches down to open it and removes the familiar envelope, the one he left on the nightstand at the hospital. The one that contains our divorce papers.

He straightens, takes the papers out of the envelope, then sets them on the desk. He moves to stand behind me.

I stare down at the stack as he closes his hands over mine and kisses my neck.

"What is this?" I ask, turning my head a little.

"Time for you to choose what you want."

I study him.

He smiles, reaches into his pocket, and sets something on top of the papers.

I shift my gaze to find our wedding rings. Well, slightly different. Two platinum bands, the black diamond bands gone, the blood diamond set in a modern, clean, and beautiful setting for me.

I swallow and shift my gaze back to his.

"You choose. Sign them now or tear them up. Tear them up and marry me, Cristina. Marry me right. No dead roses. No thorns. And no ghosts to haunt our future."

EPILOGUE 2
DAMIAN

One Year Later

Michela watches her son proudly. She looks good. California agrees with her. Or it's the man at her side I only met a few minutes ago that's put a little color back in her face. I've already got Tobias looking into who he is.

Bennie is my best man. He's nearly ten and I hate that I only see him a few times a year. But it's what Michela wants, and I'll give her the space she needs. For now. I've given her share of the Di Santo inheritance back to her but am managing Bennie's trust myself. A backup plan just in case she decides to cut me out entirely.

Cristina's aunt and Simona sit in the pew opposite Michela's. It's a small wedding. Neither of us really has any friends.

The music changes and a hush falls over the church. It's time.

The double doors open, letting in a bright white light.

I turn.

Standing in the doorway with that light behind her, Cristina looks like an angel. Like she's been sent from heaven above.

My heartbeat kicks up as she takes a step inside. The doors close. And I'm in awe.

She is stunning in her wedding dress. A proper wedding dress this time. A snow-white lace gown cut close to hug her body and fanning out below her knees to touch the floor. In her hands, she holds a single long-stemmed red rose. No thorns. The red matches the color of her lips.

From behind the floor-length veil, violet eyes lined with smoky black, lock with mine.

She is fierce, my bride.

Different than the last time we did this.

She walks alone down the aisle. Liam was supposed to escort her to me, but he took off a few months ago. I know she's worried about him. I am too, honestly. But I just got a location. I haven't told her that yet. I plan on paying him a visit myself first to encourage him to get his head out of his ass before he gets hurt.

Clearing my throat, I focus my eyes on her. The music and the faces in the pews fade from my periphery as I take her in.

My wife. My bride. My love.

No bridesmaids for her. No girlfriends to speak of, even considering school. But I think that's how she is. Who she is.

We're the same in this, she and I. And we're closer for it.

I smile when she reaches the altar. When I lift her veil to look into her eyes, I see the vulnerability alongside that ferocity. The strength she's always had. I never doubted it, not even in the beginning. She wouldn't have survived me if she'd not been strong.

"You're beautiful," I say.

She smiles and a tear slips from her eye. I watch it make its way down her cheek, and when a second one follows, I cup her face and pull her to me gently. I lay a soft kiss where that tear is, and when I do, she turns her face a little, just enough to lay her cheek against mine.

I slide my hands down her arms and interlace my fingers with hers. That single rose drops to our feet. I smell the soft scent of her perfume, feel the smooth skin of her cheek.

"I'm nervous," she whispers.

I draw back, set my forehead against hers, and we lock eyes.

"Don't be. This is right. *We* are right. I've got you."

"I know you do."

"And I love you."

"I love you, Damian."

The end

SAMPLE FROM TAKEN
HELENA

I'm the oldest of the Willow quadruplets. Four girls. Always girls. Every single quadruplet birth, generation after generation, it's always girls.

This generation's crop yielded the usual, but instead of four perfect, beautiful dolls, there were three.

And me.

And today, our twenty-first birthday, is the day of harvesting.

That's the Scafoni family's choice of words, not ours. At least not mine. My parents seem much more comfortable with it than my sisters and I do, though.

Harvesting is always on the twenty-first birthday of the quads. I don't know if it's written in stone somewhere or what, but it's what I know and what has been on the back of my mind since I learned our history five years ago.

There's an expression: *those who cannot remember the past are condemned to repeat it.* Well, that's bullshit, because we Willows know well our past and look at us now.

The same blocks that have been used for centuries standing in the old library, their surfaces softened by the feet of every other Willow Girl who stood on the same stumps of wood, and all I can think when I see them, the four lined up like they are, is how archaic this is, how fucking unreal. How they can't do this to us.

Yet, here we are.

And they are doing this to us.

But it's not *us*, really.

My shift is marked.

I'm *unclean*.

So it's really my sisters.

Sometimes I'm not sure who I hate more, my own family for allowing this insanity generation after generation, or the Scafoni monsters for demanding the sacrifice.

"It's time," my father says. His voice is grave.

He's aged these last few months. I wonder if that's remorse because it certainly isn't backbone.

I heard he and my mother argue once, exactly once, and then it was over.

He simply accepted it.

Accepted that tonight, his daughters will be made to stand on those horrible blocks while a Scafoni bastard looks us over, prods and pokes us, maybe checks our teeth like you would a horse, before making his choice. Before taking one of my sisters as his for the next three years of her life.

I'm not naive enough to be unsure what that will mean exactly. Maybe my sisters are, but not me.

"Up on the block. Now, Helena."

I look at my sisters who already stand so meekly on their appointed stumps. They're all paler than usual tonight and I swear I can hear their hearts pounding in fear of what's to come.

When I don't move right away, my father painfully takes my arm and lifts me up onto my block and all I can think, the one thing that gives me the slightest hope, is that if Sebastian Scafoni chooses me, I will find some way to end this. I won't condemn my daughters to this fate. My nieces. My granddaughters.

But he won't choose me, and I think that's why my parents are angrier than usual with me.

See, I'm the ugly duckling. At least I'd be considered ugly standing next to my sisters.

And the fact that I'm unclean—not a virgin—means I won't be taken.

The Scafoni bastard will choose one of their precious golden daughters instead.

Golden, to my dark. Golden—quite literally. Sparkling almost, my sisters.

I glance at them as my father attaches the iron shackle to my ankle. He doesn't do this to any of them. They'll do as they're told, even as their gazes bounce from the closed twelve-foot doors to me and back again and again and again.

But I have no protection to offer. Not tonight. Not on this one.

The backs of my eyes burn with tears I refuse to shed.

"How can you do this? How can you allow it?" I ask for the hundredth time. I'm talking to my mother while my father clasps the restraints on my wrists, making sure I won't attack the monsters.

"Better gag her, too."

It's my mother's response to my question and, a moment later, my father does as he's told and ensures my silence.

I hate my mother more, I think. She's a Willow quadruplet. She witnessed a harvesting herself. Witnessed the result of this cruel tradition.

Tradition.

A tradition of kidnapping.

Of breaking.

Of destroying.

I look to my sisters again. Three almost carbon copies of each other, with long blonde hair curling around their shoulders, flowing down their backs, their blue eyes wide with fear.

Well, except in Julia's case.

She's different than the others. She's more... eager. But I don't think she has a clue what they'll do to her.

Me, no one would guess I came from the same batch.

Opposite their gold, my hair is so dark a black, it appears almost blue, with one single, wide streak of silver to relieve the stark shade, a flaw I was born with. And contrasting their cornflower-blue eyes, mine are a midnight sky; there too, the only relief the silver specks that dot them.

They look like my mother. Like perfect dolls.

I look like my great-aunt, also named Helena, down to the silver streak I refuse to dye. She's in her nineties now. I wonder if they had to lock her in her room and steal her wheelchair, so she wouldn't interfere in the ceremony.

Aunt Helena was the chosen girl of her generation. She knows what's in store for us better than anyone.

"They're coming," my mother says.

She has super hearing, I swear, but then, a moment later, I hear them too.

A door slams beyond the library, and the draft blows out a dozen of the thousand candles that light the huge room.

A maid rushes to relight them. No electricity. Tradition, I guess.

If I were Sebastian Scafoni, I'd want to get a good look at the prize I'd be fucking for the next year. And I have no doubt there will be fucking, because what else can break a girl so completely but taking that of all things?

And it's not just the one year. No. We're given for three years. One year for each brother. Oldest to youngest. It used to be four, but now, it's three.

I would pinch my arm to be sure I'm really standing here, that I'm not dreaming, but my hands are bound behind my back, and I can't.

This can't be fucking real. It can't be legal.

And yet here we are, the four of us, naked beneath our translucent, rotting sheaths—I swear I smell the decay on them—standing on our designated blocks, teetering on them. I guess the Willows of the past had smaller feet. And I admit, as I hear their heavy, confident footfalls approaching the ancient wooden doors of the library, I am afraid.

I'm fucking terrified.

One-Click Taken now!

Thank you for reading *Unholy Intent*, the final book of the *Unholy Union Duet*. I hope you loved Damian and Cristina's story and would consider leaving a review in the store where you purchased the books.

If you'd like to sign up for my newsletter and keep up to date on new books, sales and events, click here! I don't ever share your information and promise not to clog up your inbox.

Like my FB Author Page to keep updated on news and giveaways!

I have a FB Fan Group where I share exclusive teasers, giveaways and just fun stuff. Probably TMI :) It's called The Knight Spot. I'd love for you to join us! Just click here!

ALSO BY NATASHA KNIGHT

Unholy Union Duet

Unholy Union
Unholy Intent

Collateral Damage Duet

Collateral: an Arranged Marriage Mafia Romance
Damage: an Arranged Marriage Mafia Romance

Ties that Bind Duet

Mine
His

Dark Legacy Trilogy

Taken (Dark Legacy, Book 1)
Torn (Dark Legacy, Book 2)
Twisted (Dark Legacy, Book 3)

MacLeod Brothers

Devil's Bargain

Benedetti Mafia World

Salvatore: a Dark Mafia Romance

Dominic: a Dark Mafia Romance

Sergio: a Dark Mafia Romance

The Benedetti Brothers Box Set (Contains Salvatore, Dominic and Sergio)

Killian: a Dark Mafia Romance

Giovanni: a Dark Mafia Romance

The Amado Brothers

Dishonorable

Disgraced

Unhinged

Standalone Dark Romance

Descent

Deviant

Beautiful Liar

Retribution

Theirs To Take

Captive, Mine

Alpha

Given to the Savage

Taken by the Beast

Claimed by the Beast

Captive's Desire

Protective Custody

Amy's Strict Doctor

Taming Emma

Taming Megan

Taming Naia

Reclaiming Sophie

The Firefighter's Girl

Dangerous Defiance

Her Rogue Knight

Taught To Kneel

Tamed: the Roark Brothers Trilogy

ACKNOWLEDGMENTS

Cover Design by CoverLuv

Editing by Editing4Indies

ABOUT THE AUTHOR

USA Today bestselling author of contemporary romance, Natasha Knight specializes in dark, tortured heroes. Happily-Ever-Afters are guaranteed, but she likes to put her characters through hell to get them there. She's evil like that.

Want more?
www.natasha-knight.com
natasha-knight@outlook.com